WAVES OF MURDER

WAVES OF MURDER

A Fiona Quinn Mystery

C.S. McDonald

ISBN: 0991368096
ISBN 13: 9780991368099
Library of Congress Control Number: 2017904589
McWriter Books, Hookstown, PA

One

Ribbons of sunlight danced through the leaves of the magnolia tree like regretful whispers of good-bye. Stroking her long silky hair, Harrison looked into Abigail's violet eyes. "I wish this war was over. I wish it had never begun. I wish I could stay here under the cool shade of the magnolia and kiss your lips for as long as I please. But I must go. Those wretched yanks have burned Atlanta to the ground, and I must join our men to rescue what is left of the South."

"Please, Harrison. Please don't go. I need you. I need you so much. So many of our neighbors have gone, never to return, and those who have come home are battered and broken." She pressed her lips to his, desperately trying to keep him in her loving embrace—far from harm's way.

Letting out an indifferent sigh, Fiona Quinn raked her fingers through her strawberry blond hair. "Well, it's about time you did *something*, Harrison. You've been nothing but a blood-sucking gold digger since Abigail met you in chapter two. I can't believe her father let you onto the plantation in the first place. Then again, her father was murdered in chapter three—I bet that little weasel, Harrison, did it," Fiona grumbled, as she

1

rubbed her eyes, turned her laptop off, and checked her text messages for the thousandth time—nothing. At this point, she would give anything—*anything* at all for an honest distraction from the manuscript she was editing for best-selling romance author, Wyla Parkes.

The manuscript was the first book of a four-book anthology. The books would follow Abigail Wentworth, then her daughters and granddaughters through their volatile relationships from the Civil War to WWII, and maybe farther. Wyla hadn't decided yet.

Pushing to her feet, Fiona stretched her back. She went into the bedroom and opened the nightstand drawer to retrieve a candy bar from her stash. Letting out yet another apathetic sigh, she unwrapped the Three Musketeers bar. Hey, she deserved the chocolate rush—Lord knew she needed it. Over the past six and a half hours, she'd been pouring over the manuscript, reading words like, alas, hence, and fraught. Seriously? Who would use the word fraught? Evidently, Wyla Parkes and her heroine Abigail Wentworth use those words. Fiona wasn't a big fan of romance books—she preferred edgy suspense thrillers. When the calendar drew near to Halloween, she was always up for a little Stephen King. On a cold winter's night, an Agatha Christie mystery would suit her fancy while she sat wrapped in a cozy blanket, sipping hot chocolate.

Usually, Fiona's mother would edit Wyla's manuscripts—Nancy Quinn was the author's trusted long-time friend. Fiona's mother and Wyla had gone to high school together and were college roommates as well. Nancy, who had a degree in literature, would travel to Presque Isle every summer and spend at least six weeks editing Wyla's latest work. Only over the next six weeks, she was having cataract surgery in both eyes, making the trip and the editing impossible. Wyla was disappointed. Fiona's mom volunteered her for the job.

Fiona wasn't happy about the arrangement. She was a kindergarten teacher in Pittsburgh and she had been looking forward to summer recess. She wanted to get a jump on some much-needed painting in her house. There was always plenty of yardwork, and she was looking forward to spending extra time with her boyfriend, Nathan Landry, who was a detective for the Pittsburgh police, homicide division.

"You can't pass up this opportunity, Fiona Nicole. Wyla will pay you a boatload of money, and the accommodations are beautiful," her mother said when she called to tell her that she'd offered up Fiona's services—and time.

"I have other plans for my summer, Mom."

"I already told her that you were coming. You can't turn down this kind of money—you'll need it for when you and Nathan get *married*."

Fiona sighed so loudly that she was certain her mother could feel the roll of her eyes across the phone connection. "Seriously, I don't understand why I actually need to *go to* her beach house. It's the twenty-first century for crying out loud. If all the editing is being done on a computer and then emailed to her, why can't I do it from here?"

"Not Wyla's style. She prefers her editor to be right there, on hand, so she can discuss changes in the manuscript with you personally. It's just the way she is—you know how creative people can be…very…*eccentric*. Believe me, Wyla Parkes could probably teach a class on eccentricity."

Thusly (one of those words Fiona couldn't imagine anyone in the twenty-first century using) she was obligated for the next six weeks to edit at least two, but hopefully, three of the books from the anthology that had been titled, *Waves of Romance*.

Ugh.

She bit into the chocolatey gooey Three Musketeers bar. Yum.

A breeze swept through the sliding glass doors that opened onto a darling veranda with a gorgeous view of Lake Erie. She looked out to see her white Maltese, Harriet, curled up on one of the overstuffed blue and white striped cushions on the white wicker chairs. Harriet seemed to love the lake. She spent most of her time sleeping out on the veranda as Fiona worked on the manuscript. Like a comforting lullaby, the waves gently lapped over the sand of the private beach where Wyla's huge house was located.

Staying at the beach house was a fabulous perk—along with a fabulous paycheck. Truly, Fiona really didn't have much to complain about. Wyla didn't bother her too much as Fiona was staying in a small guest cottage located across the main driveway from the house. She had her own kitchen, living room, two small bedrooms, bathroom, laundry, a beautiful veranda, and her own small garage to park her Mini Cooper. Wyla had no qualms about Fiona bringing Harriet along. Nice. Still, she would've rather spent her summer painting, weeding, and spending time with Nathan.

"No worries," Nathan said when she informed him of her impending six-week obligation. "I'll come to visit on my days off. It'll be fun. We'll spend time on the beach, we can go biking, and maybe I can get a little fishing in."

"I'm not comfortable with my house being empty for so long. When I go on vacation, I'm not usually gone for more than a week at a time," she said.

"Don't be such a worry-wort, Fi. I'll check in on your house, and I'll bring your mail along when I come to visit. It's all good."

To be honest, she wasn't really worried about her house being empty. She was more concerned about Nathan checking in on the house—because it wasn't empty. It was never empty—even during the days when Fiona was at school. Truth was her late grandmother,

Evelyn, lived in the house. Fiona had purchased the family home from her parents when they retired from teaching and moved to Florida several years ago. When she was living, Evelyn resided in the third-floor apartment of the Quinn's home at 529 Oxford Street. After her death, she remained. Evelyn looked after Fiona—she was her guardian grandmother, and in turn, Fiona felt she looked after Evelyn's spirit by keeping the house so she would feel comfortable staying there. She was Evelyn's guardian granddaughter. Their uncanny arrangement worked—in a strange and wonderful way, it worked.

Evelyn was known to move things around in the house. She made coffee every morning—which was a superb ethereal perk, but with Fiona gone, what would she do with Nathan coming in and out of the house? Would she behave or would she take the opportunity to play some ghostly tricks? Yeah, Evelyn could be like that.

Feeling she'd suffered through enough of Abigail Wentworth's romantic tragedies for one day, Fiona stepped out onto the veranda to breathe in the evening breeze. The sun was just beginning to set over the lake. Long wide swaths of purple and pink edged the horizon of the water, while the fiery sun made its descent seemingly right into the rolling whitecaps. Beautiful. She eased down on a chair and gathered Harriet onto her lap to relax and take in the splendor of the lake.

Muffled voices coming from the distance interrupted her attempt to finish off her candy. Harriet raised her head and perked her ears at the sudden sound of conversation. Holding the Maltese close to her chest, Fiona stood and craned her neck to look beyond the arches that corralled the veranda to see a man and a woman on the beach. The woman wore a purple retro Bohemian-style caftan and a wide-brimmed beach hat. The flowing sleeves of her tunic flapped in the wind, while the yards of fabric that made up the dress sucked against her long lean body.

Over the sounds of the waves and the wind, she couldn't make out what they were saying, but it was obvious by the intensity of their tone and body language that they were definitely arguing.

The woman waved her arms at the man, while he shook his head at her, kicking sand with the tip of his shoe, and pressing his hands into the pockets of his light brown windbreaker. Irritation defining her every move, she turned to shuffle away from him through the deep sand. Obviously frustrated, the man followed.

Fiona stretched and strained to see who they might be when the woman's hat blew from her head to reveal her identity—it was Wyla. Her dark bobbed hair whipped in the breeze as she continued her heated march across the beach toward the house. The man chased her hat, managing to capture it just before it reached the water's edge.

"Wyla, wait!" he called to her as he picked up his pace to a jog, but she didn't acknowledge his cries at all, as they both drew closer to the house. "Please, Wyla—we can make this work if you'll just hear me out!"

Hokay, that was quite enough.

Fiona hurried into the cottage, sliding the door closed. She didn't want Wyla or the man to know she'd seen or heard anything. Wyla's business was none of her business, and she didn't want the author to think her editor was poking her nose where it simply did not belong. Still, she had to wonder who the man was. Perhaps a lover or ex-husband? A business associate? Or could he be an author? Was Wyla Parkes life always filled with drama or was she a femme fatale? The rocky relationship scenario made perfect sense. After all, Wyla was a romance author—she had to draw from something to come up with her story lines, right?

Perhaps Wyla's love life was just as tragic as Abigail Wentworth's. Then again, the man seemed fairly upset over their argument—maybe she was the source of tragedy in men's lives. Hm. Possibly over the coming weeks she'd witness more of the woman's entanglements. Hey, the editing job may prove to be more interesting than she thought.

"When this is all said and done—I may be able to write a book!" Fiona told Harriet.

The next morning didn't provide ribbons of sunlight through anything—it was full blown sunshine in the big sky shimmering over the lake, making the whitecaps look like sparkling gems rolling toward the shore.

Before starting her long day at the laptop, Fiona decided she was going to put on her new red bathing suit, spread a blanket over the sand, and bask in the sun for an hour or two. While Harriet danced around her ankles, Fiona plopped her wide-brimmed hat on her head, grabbed her coffee and blanket, and then made her way to the private beach just beyond the veranda.

She no sooner got comfortable on her blanket when terse voices wafted down from the balcony of the beach house.

"You've broken your promise to him, Wyla. I can't believe you don't understand why he's so upset. I'm just as upset as he is. You've broken our trust as well. I don't understand. What's going on with you?" a man's voice demanded.

Unlike last night, Fiona had no problem hearing the conversation. Wyla and her guest were a short distance above her, and they were not making any attempt to keep their voices down.

Did she dare a look to see if it was the same man from the beach last evening or was it someone else whose feathers had been ruffled by the famous author?

Fiona figured that they were unaware of her presence or surely they'd move their conversation inside. Slowly, as not to be detected, she moved her body to the other end of the blanket so her face was toward the house, her back to the lake. She lay down flat. At this point, she had a great view of the balcony. Thinking she was playing some sort of game, Harriet jumped around her. She nipped and licked playfully at Fiona's nose.

"No, no, not now, Harriet," Fiona whispered while batting the dog away from her face. Unaffected by her mistress's reprimand, Harriet simply ran off to bite and bound at the water splashing to the shore.

Fiona turned her attention to Wyla sitting at a table sporting a different caftan than she wore last evening—it was a soft aqua color with big yellow flowers. *How many of those does Wyla have? They look comfortable enough. Maybe I should search the internet for one.*

The man sitting across from Wyla was not the same man she'd argued with the night before. Even though he was seated, this man looked to be much taller than the other. He had a nest of thick grey hair, and he wore a pair of red-rimmed glasses, which made him look dignified in a fresh sort of manner.

Wyla sipped from a dainty teacup and then set it down. "You publishers are all alike. You think I should bow to your every whim. You think I should hand over every piece of work that I—*Wyla Parkes*—creates.

Well, not this time. I told you, I've decided to publish Waves of Romance independently, and that's that. I'm sorry that you and Sam feel cheated, or betrayed in some way, but I've made my decision."

"Is this some kind of ploy to get more royalties, Wyla? We've been good to you. You've made a lot of money over the years. You live in this beautiful beach house. The last time I checked, you drive a very expensive car, and I know how you love to shop. We've even let you hire your own editor—you know how that goes against our better judgment. No other author under our umbrella is allowed to hire a private editor."

"Nancy does a beautiful job. Much better than *your* editors. Early in my career, when you had control over that, I'd find as many as two errors in my published works. Negotiating to bring Nancy aboard was brilliant on my part. And need I remind you, when you signed me on, your publishing company was a struggling baby learning to crawl—my romance novels put you on the map." Clasping her hands together, she leaned forward over the table. "Please, Lester, let me do this. I need to try. So many authors are doing a little self-pubbing nowadays. I need a new adventure in my life. I'm afraid I'm getting stale in my older years."

Taking his coffee mug with him, the man pushed away from the table. From Fiona's vantage point, it looked as though he was trying to gather up his patience. He wandered over to the railing and leaned a hip against it. He stared into his mug as if he would find the right words swirling in his coffee. He said, "You—stale? Never. You haven't signed a contract with us for this anthology, we'd love to have it of course. But…if this is truly what you want, I'll respect your wishes. I don't know if Sam will—that's his business. But—as your publisher, I must remind you that Noble Press owns the name Wyla Parkes. You won't be able to publish this work under that name. I hope you realize whatever pen name you decide upon will be unknown to your readers. You'll have to grow an audience for your new work. Isn't it a bit late in your career for that nonsense?"

"Maybe. But I want to try." She let out a beleaguered sigh. "Now that we've ironed that all out, you should go. I have writing to do, and you're holding me up. Oh! And I need to come up with a snappy pen name," Wyla said.

The man kissed her hand. "There's only one Wyla Parkes—and that's all there ever will be."

The room was growing darker. Abigail grew weaker by the moment. She feared she could never hold on until Harrison returned. Would he return? She'd fought so hard, so very hard, and she'd been waiting too long. She felt the cool water drip down her temples from the cloth

gently pressed to her head. She could barely open her eyes, but she knew it was her dear daughter, Tarah who held the compress. She'd been staying by her side through it all—unlike her husband, Carlton, or her older daughter, Elizabeth. They'd abandoned her long ago—before the bitter war took everything they had.

"Am I too late?" she heard a man say. His voice sounded so far away, and yet it was so familiar. Could it be?

She felt her daughter's weight lift from the bed. Tarah said, "Harrison...I thought you'd never come back. We believed you to be dead, and then I heard you'd married—" She hesitated. Her voice grew angrier. "I prayed that you were dead. I prayed you'd never return. As much as I hate the very sight of you, Mother needs you now."

Suddenly his warm hands were upon her clammy skin. His breath feathered her face. "Abigail...I'm so sorry it has taken so long to return. I'm here now, and I want you to know that I will love you forever—"

Those were the very words she had waited to hear, but alas it was too late—there was no time left. No time—but at least they were the last words she would listen to as her weary eyes closed.

The End

Finally! Finally, Fiona had reached the end of the first manuscript. It was also the end of her first week at Wyla Parkes's beach house. She looked up at the clock, it was three-thirty—not too bad. After making sure her track changes to the manuscript were properly recorded and saved, she emailed the edited manuscript to Wyla. She still had no idea why she couldn't have simply edited the manuscript from her home in Pittsburgh. Over the past week, she'd had very little contact with Wyla. She could've accomplished her summer projects and in the interim, Wyla would've gotten her manuscript edited—it would've been a win/win situation for both.

Whatever.

Tomorrow she would rest her eyes and her brain—spend some time lying on the beach. Honestly, she wasn't sure how much more she could take of Wyla's mushy romance novels.

Yeesh.

The good news was that tomorrow was Friday—Nathan had the weekend off and would be coming to Presque Isle to visit. She couldn't wait to see him. She'd been feeling so isolated in the cottage, practically handcuffed to the laptop, with no one to talk to. She planned to take a nice long walk along the beach with Harriet later in the evening—maybe at sunset. Hopefully, a quiet stroll in the sand would help to clear her mind of the tortured southern belle, Abigail Wentworth.

Rushing from the shower, Fiona wrapped her white robe tautly around her body. She struggled to keep the towel twisted about her wet hair from falling off her head. Someone was ringing the doorbell at the sliding glass doors. As she trotted down the short hallway, she could see Wyla standing on the veranda holding a box in her hands. Peering through the glass, she was obviously trying to figure out if Fiona was in the cottage. Harriet was staring back at her with her head cocked to the side. She wasn't barking, it seemed she was trying to decide who the woman was. Sometimes her little white fluffy security system malfunctioned. Clearly, this was one of those moments.

Wyla was still wearing the aqua and yellow floral caftan—she wore it well, along with the grey streak of hair precisely placed to cascade around the right side of her face. Her gold hoop earrings dangled just below her chin. She was an elegant older woman. With one last tug at the sash of her robe, Fiona slid the door open.

Wyla gasped. "Oh! I'm so sorry. I've caught you at a bad time."

"Not at all," Fiona said. "I just stepped out of the shower."

She handed Fiona the box that was tied up with string. It was a bakery box "I wanted to bring these to you. They are absolutely luscious chocolate truffles. The man who owns the bakery on State Street is always bringing me the most mouthwatering cookies and cakes. He lives up the beach about a mile. I think he thinks I'll go out with him—either that or he wants to see how fat he can make me. I'm hoping he's interested in a date—he's quite good-looking. Actually, there are a couple men in the beach neighborhood who look very interesting, but at least this one comes with skills—baking skills."

Fiona chuckled. "Thank you, my boyfriend is coming to visit this weekend. You just saved me from having to come up with some treats, but just in case, what's the name of this bakery? I might be making a last minute run."

"Mm, Belford's Bakery...or maybe Bellaire Bakery—no, no, that's the name of a hotel nearby. What's wrong with me? I can't remember. I guess my mind has been on other things. Oh! It's *Belafonte's* Bakery. The owner's name is Tony. Now that I think about it, his name must be Tony Belafonte. Anyway, mention my name—he might give you a discount."

"I will, thanks again. Did you get my edits?"

"I did. Good girl, you had lots of them. That's the sign of a good editor. If there are very few corrections or suggestions, the editor isn't worth the time. Of course, I haven't gotten through all of them yet, but I did glance through. Did you enjoy the story?"

Fiona gulped. She could feel a warm flush rising on her cheeks, and she hoped Wyla hadn't noticed. "Oh,

yes, I enjoyed it *very* much. That Abigail, she's really…
something."

Wyla's eyes brightened. "You liked it? I'm surprised.
Your mother absolutely *hates* my stories."

Fiona blinked back. "What? Really? Why does she
edit for you?"

Wyla waved a dismissive hand. "Editing has nothing to do with if you like romance, or suspense, or mysteries. It's all about looking for corrections or reworking
sentences or finding a hole in the author's story." She
laughed. "Nancy makes fun of my stories—she says
they're too mushy. Hey, sex sells, I always tell her. She
mostly comes for the wine and the friendship, I think."

"I see."

"Anyway, I'll be looking over what you've done
starting tonight. I'll be making changes to the manuscript over the weekend—I have already added a few
rewrites. I'll sit down with you to discuss the changes
and some of your recommendations on Monday. Get
ready! You'll be reworking that manuscript most of next
week before moving on to book two of the anthology.
I'm sure you've already guessed, it'll be *Tarah's* story.
Well, enjoy the truffles and your weekend with your
beau. I hope you'll bring him over to the house to
introduce me. Your mother told me he's a detective.
How very intriguing."

"I suppose it is. Would you like a cup of tea?" Fiona
asked.

"Thank you, no." She glanced over her shoulder through the glass doors. She seemed apprehensive. "I'm going to take a walk along the beach. I usually do that at sunset, but not tonight. It'll be getting dark soon enough, so I'll see you later, Fiona. If you talk to your mother, tell her I said hello."

"I'll do that." Fiona sighed. Yep, she figured Tarah would be the next story—she could hardly wait. Not!

—∿—

"C'mon, Harriet! The sun is just starting to set. Let's go for a walk. I'm so ready to get out of this tiny cottage. I swear the walls are closing in on me," Fiona said.

Harriet leapt from her comfy spot on the bed and scurried to the glass door as quickly as her short little legs would carry her. She danced and barked and jumped until Fiona finally slid the door open, and then she dashed across the veranda onto the sandy shoreline.

"Hey! Wait for me!" Fiona called after her while grabbing the leash from the hook just inside the door.

It was another spectacular sunset over the lake. Deep hues of purple, and pink, and blazing red painted the sky over the gently rolling waters. Fiona figured they had at least an hour of daylight left before darkness would drape the beach. She wasn't terribly worried—there had been a full moon last night. A walk in the moonlight might be refreshing—she planned to walk the beach tomorrow night hand in hand with Nathan. How romantic. She couldn't wait.

The seagulls flew just over the water, dipping into the tarn every now and then. Their squawks blended with the sound of the waves rolling and crashing to the shore—it was the unceasing symphony of the lake.

Fiona walked along laughing at Harriet trying to outrun the water as it swept up onto the sand. Looking down, she realized that someone else must've been taking their dog for a walk—very recently. Two sets of footprints—one human and one canine were slowly washing away with the rising of the tide. The beaches in this area didn't tend to be very busy—they were privately owned. She scanned the shoreline to see a woman wearing a ball cap, a pair of shorts, and a racerback tank jogging over the next hill, a dog running alongside her. The dog's collar gleamed as the setting sun shot its final rays across the beach. They were far ahead and would soon drop over the sandy rise out of sight.

Evidently, she wasn't the only one who thought it was a perfect evening for a walk or a jog along the lake.

Just ahead, she noticed something glimmering in the sand. As she drew closer, she could see that it was an earring—a gold hoop. She bent down to pick it up only to see another glimmering item in the sand about fifteen feet ahead. She didn't have to walk very far to see that it was another golden hoop. She stilled, examining the earring in her hand—it looked just like the earrings Wyla had been wearing when she visited earlier—around seven. Perhaps she'd lost them as she was taking her walk.

How strange.

To lose one earring would be normal—it could've become dislodged and fallen from her lobe. But to lose both earrings? The author didn't strike Fiona as someone who would wear cheap jewelry that would unsnap easily.

Again—strange.

Harriet growled and barked, causing Fiona to flinch from her musing. She looked up to see her Maltese snarling while backing away from the water's edge.

The water lapped heavily against the shore.

Fiona inched toward her dog and the surf.

Harriet continued to growl and whine, while looking at her mistress, then to the water, and back at Fiona.

The closer Fiona came to the water's edge, the more she could see yellow and aqua fabric bobbing in the current, floating on the surface. Plumes of fabric filled with air bubbles mounded above the water.

She gulped back what she feared she was about to see when Wyla Parkes's body rolled onto the sand.

Gasping, Fiona took several steps backward and then, mustering all the courage she had, she took a step forward. It was too late. There was nothing she could do for Wyla—it was most obvious she was dead.

Fiona looked up. The woman and her dog had disappeared from sight. How could the woman not have seen Wyla? She searched the sand, but the last of the woman's and dog's footprints had already washed away. The lake had quaffed any sign that they'd been there. Fumbling frantically in her pocket for her cell phone, Fiona had to wonder—was the woman jogging or was she running away? As the phone connected her to the 9-1-1 operator, she was trying to remember details about the woman: black shorts, a lime green tank, ball cap—what color was the cap? She couldn't recall. What kind of dog was with her? Yellow lab—no, a Golden Retriever, maybe. Or was it one of those Golden Doodles? She knew it had a shimmery collar.

What did the woman witness, or worse...what did the woman do?

TWO

Everything had worked out perfectly. After a three-day investigation, Detective Nathan Landry managed to get the latest suspect to confess to killing his lifelong best friend over a horse-racing wager. Nice guy. Anyway, the situation was in the hands of the justice system. He was done. He'd filed his report. His desk was clear, and he was free to head for Presque Isle to visit Fiona an entire day before he'd planned to go. He would arrive late, but she would be surprised and they would be able to spend a little extra time together. He couldn't wait to see her.

The sun was setting when Nathan rolled his Honda CRV to a stop in front of Fiona's house. As promised, he would make sure the house was secure and collect the mail to take to her.

After shutting off the engine, he looked up at the house—the porch light was on, again. How was that possible? When he stopped by the house on Wednesday, he made sure he'd turned the light off, but there it was—shining into the dark.

He tapped his fingers on the steering wheel.

From the outside, the house didn't look at all creepy. The house at 529 Oxford Street looked just like any of the houses located in the older neighborhoods of Pittsburgh. It was a brick, four-story house with a basement, a main floor, a second floor, and a third-floor attic—which had been an apartment at one time or other. Nope, there was nothing particularly weird or off about the house that Fiona had grown up in. Yet when he'd been in the house gathering her mail from the foyer floor just below the mail slot, the house made some strange sounds. He heard peculiar movements. When he walked through the home, nothing was out of place, everything seemed fine. Surely, the sound and the movement was just his imagination—or perhaps the shifting sounds that older houses tend to make.

Nathan got out of his SUV to make his way up the sidewalk and across the porch. After unlocking the door, he carefully stepped inside. He was certain there would be another round of mail scattered over the floor beneath the mail slot. On Wednesday, he'd picked up all the mail and stacked it neatly on the first step of the stairs. He figured he'd collect the whole weeks' worth of mail when he was ready to go to Erie—that way he wouldn't lose anything that may be important in the mess he tended to have in his car.

Sure enough, when he pushed the door open there was mail scattered about the floor. He stepped over the envelopes and brochures and began to gather them all together when he noticed the pile he'd stacked on the stairs from Wednesday was no longer one pile—it was three. Still bent over, Nathan stopped mid-chore. His eyes narrowed. Straightening from his stooped over position, he made his way over to the staircase and the three piles of mail lying on the first step. The small stacks were neatly lined up and organized. Pile one consisted of bills—Fiona's electric bill, the cable bill, and a water bill. The second pile was made up of flyers and brochures—one from Pittsburgh Ballet Theater, another from a cruise line, and two from department stores with coupons. The third pile had magazines that Fiona evidently subscribed to—Good Housekeeping and Cosmopolitan.

Baffled, Nathan rubbed the nape of his neck. Who else had a key to Fiona's house? Did she have someone else checking the house besides him? Did she not trust him? Wait…maybe Fiona's brother, Chad, had been checking on the house as well. Still…organizing the mail in piles? That didn't seem like Chad's style. It seemed to Nathan that Chad would have trouble organizing his socks into pairs. The young man just didn't come off as that focused.

Studying the piles of mail, he wondered what happened to all the junk mail he'd collected from the floor on Wednesday. After glancing around the small foyer, he found the answer. The junk mail was stuffed into a small waste bin that sat beside a decorative table against the wall. Yeah, that totally disqualified Chad from the scenario—there was no way he'd care enough about the junk mail to get rid of it.

"Well, I guess I should separate the mail accordingly and add it to the piles," Nathan said to himself as he set to placing bills on the first pile, brochures on the second, and a sales catalog from a department store on the third—would that be considered junk mail? To him—yes. To a woman—probably not. He figured he'd best file it with the others on pile number two.

He gathered the three piles and made them into one for ease of carrying to the car when he heard noises coming from the second floor—it sounded like someone was walking around up there, and then there was a loud *thump*. He set the compiled mail on the step, turned off the porch light, and then stealthily made his way up the staircase.

Moving cautiously from one room to the next, Nathan found nothing had been disturbed on the second floor—the bedrooms, and Fiona's computer room were just as they'd been on Wednesday when he made the same trek through the house.

He stopped when he came to the door that led to the third-floor apartment where Fiona told him her grandmother used to live. He hadn't gone up there on Wednesday. Surely no one was hiding on the third floor. As much as he simply wanted to grab the mail and leave for Erie, Nathan figured he should check—better safe than sorry.

He opened the door that led to the attic to find a stair lift still attached to the wall. The enclosed staircase that was located directly above the main staircase smelled musty. Furtively, he climbed the stairs listening for anything suspicious. When he reached the top he found living room furniture covered in sheets, a bed, a dresser, and an antique-looking desk near one of the windows. The room appeared to be trapped in a time from years gone by. The large open space smelled as musty as the stairs, but as the rest of the house, nothing seemed to be amiss.

Nathan made his way back to the main staircase and as he descended toward the main floor, he came to a complete halt. He immediately noticed that his single pile of mail had once again been separated into three piles. When he reached the piles he could see that they were exactly as he'd found them when he'd arrived—a pile of Fiona's bills, brochures, and magazines. The mail he'd collected from the floor when he arrived had been added to the appropriate pile.

What the heck is going on? Nathan looked up to see that the switch for the porch light had been turned back on.

"Now I know I turned that off, for sure," he muttered, as he swatted the switch into the off position again.

Nathan had no idea what was going on in Fiona's house, but he was certain of one thing, he was ready to leave. After once again gathering up the mail into one pile, he closed and locked the door, and then made his way to his vehicle. Tossing the mail onto the passenger seat, he gave the house a parting glance. The porch light flicked on.

He let out a bemused sigh. "I've got some questions for you, Fiona."

Wyla Parkes's house and the beach was a tornado of hustle. When the police arrived with sirens wailing, Fiona showed them where Wyla's body had washed up onto the shore. She gave them the earring she'd found and showed them the second earring she'd left lying in the sand—she didn't want to touch the other earring in case there was any DNA or some other physical evidence on it. She was glad she'd brought a leash along to keep Harriet at bay.

A nanosecond later, the quiet beach had transformed into a hotbed of police, ambulance, and crime investigation teams. Fiona felt as though she'd repeated her story of finding the earrings and then Wyla's dead body in the surf a dozen times to as many investigators. She was beginning to think that none of them had the ability to retain the information or their communication skills within the team were poor at best.

Finally, one of the investigators said, "Miss Quinn, thank you so much for your cooperation in this investigation, it is truly appreciated; however, I'm sure the detective will need for you to go into further detail of all the events that led up to finding Ms. Parkes' body."

"Of course," she replied. She was thankful that they'd removed Wyla's body from the water and covered her with a sheet while they waited for the coroner to arrive, she assumed.

"We have an officer who is going to take you back to the cottage where it is more comfortable to wait for the homicide detective to meet with you."

"Yes, of course."

Was that all she could think to say? She had to admit she was feeling a bit numb.

The investigator pointed to an officer waving his hand in their direction at the top of the hill. "There's the officer waiting for you. He's right up there. Do you need me to walk you up to him?"

"No...no, I see him. I'll be fine. Thank you."

Well, at least she didn't blurt out something stupid like, of course, thank you.

Fiona and Harriet were driven back to the cottage by a young officer. She figured him to be just around thirty—maybe a little older. When he opened the door for her to get out of the cruiser, and escort her to the cottage, his shoes squished with each step. The cuffs of his trousers were soaked. Fiona speculated that he'd been down near Wyla's body. Perhaps he'd been one of the first officers to respond, and his shoes filled with water when he approached the body at the water's edge.

One of the investigators looking through the cottage slid the glass door open. He said, "Please wait on the veranda, thank you." With that, he slid the door closed and pulled the vertical blinds closed.

The young officer waited with her, while in the distance more police arrived on the scene. Harriet lay at the very end of the leash watching the beach illuminated with bright flashing lights until crews showed up to set up large spotlights so the investigators and the coroner could examine Wyla's body and the surrounding area. Neon yellow crime scene tape was stretched from skinny poles the police had pounded into the sand to keep the growing crowd of onlookers back. There was a large expanse between the veranda and the crime scene—it looked like a tiny area of big movement in the distance, almost like that of a village and train under a Christmas tree, but not nearly as quaint or enjoyable.

It didn't take long at all until the investigators had split up—one group swarmed Wyla's house, another group were actively going through the cottage, while the others remained on the beach to search for any evidence the lake hadn't stolen away.

Fiona was quite sure any and all footprints from the woman and her dog were gone. Then again, perhaps the woman had nothing to do with Wyla's demise. Perhaps she'd been so preoccupied with her evening run that she totally missed the body. She couldn't imagine how, but it was possible, she guessed.

Did the man who'd argued with Wyla the night before show up for another round? Maybe their quarrel had escalated into more than whatever their issues had been.

How awful.

Fiona was certain that she would be questioned at length by the homicide detective. She was trying to remember as much as possible about the man from last evening. Her recollection triggered a slice of the crisp conversation Wyla and the man she'd called Lester were having on the balcony just that morning...

"If this is truly what you want, I'll respect it. I don't know if Sam will—that's his business." Fiona recalled the publisher telling Wyla that after their tête-à-tête had settled down to a more civil tone.

So was the Sam Lester spoke of the man on the beach arguing with Wyla the night before? Who knew? He could've been anyone, yet Wyla had told her when she stopped by the cottage that she didn't want to walk the beach at sunset. Fiona wondered, was she afraid the man would return? Was she afraid for her well-being?

Or did Wyla have drama with others—like the woman jogger for example?

Letting out a careworn sigh, Fiona didn't know what to think. After all, she didn't know Wyla very well—she was more acquainted with the author's muse, Abigail Wentworth.

Wait a minute.

Fiona was very acquainted with someone who knew Wyla extremely well—her very own mom. Maybe Mom could shed some light on the author's friends, foes, and frays. Digging into her pocket to pull out her cell phone, she felt a strong urge to call Nathan too. Hearing his soothing voice would make her feel better, and she needed him to advise her what to do or what *not* to do while being questioned.

From the edge of the veranda where he'd been leaning against an arch, texting while glancing up to watch the investigators search the beach, the police officer said, "Sorry, miss, I'm afraid I can't let you make any phone calls at this time. Not until you've been questioned by the detective."

Surprised that the officer noticed her actions, Fiona said, "Sorry." Quickly she put her cell phone back into her pocket. She snorted. "You must've pulled the short straw."

"Excuse me?"

"You've been assigned to watch me. How boring is that? You probably want to be out on the beach collecting evidence and examining the body—looking for clues, that sort of thing. Officer—"

"I'm Officer Reeves. Here's my card. You can contact me twenty-four-seven should you need me." He handed Fiona a business card, then he shrugged. "I've only been with the force for about six months. Being the new guy, I get these assignments. Goes with the territory, I guess." After giving the crime scene another glance, he returned to his texting.

Fiona filed the card in her pocket—ya never knew when you might need a cop.

The night drug on and on. The breeze from the lake became chilled. Officer Reeves allowed Fiona to fetch a sweatshirt from inside the cottage. While keeping a close eye on the activity at the crime scene on the beach, the officer followed her several times out into the sand to let Harriet relieve herself.

She wasn't sure if he felt it necessary to follow her, if he was as bored as she was, or just wanted to stretch his legs a bit. He rarely looked up from his texting, other than to check the activity at the murder scene in the distance, or to remove his shoes in an attempt to shake out the sand. Fiona couldn't blame him for texting whoever he was texting—he probably needed something to keep him alert. With droopy eyes and wide-mouthed yawns, even Harriet was starting to glance at the cottage longingly—it was getting way past the poor dog's bedtime. Fiona leaned her head back against the chair—it was past her bedtime too.

"Excuse me, Miss Quinn…hello…Miss Quinn?" a man's voice said.

Fiona flinched. Her eyes snapped open. Harriet whimpered. Raking her fingers through her hair, Fiona realized she'd fallen asleep in the chair. She looked up to find a tall, tanned, sandy-haired man standing over her. His badge, which was attached to his brown sports jacket, shined in the veranda's soft lighting. Even though she'd been snoozing, she realized he must be a cop, yet he looked more like a member of the Erie lifeguards than a police officer.

Regardless, it appeared the murder police had finally arrived to question her. She looked around. The police officer who'd been keeping watch over her was gone.

Embarrassed by her napping, while hoping there was no drool dripping down her chin, Fiona straightened in the chair, while wiping her chin—just in case. "Yes! Yes, I'm Fiona Quinn. I'm so sorry, I must've fallen asleep."

"That's understandable. It's been a long night. I'm Detective Belafonte, Erie Police."

While fluffing her hair with her fingers, she asked, "What happened to Officer Reeves?"

"He went off duty. More than likely he's at home drying his shoes or he's off to visit his girlfriend. I'd like to ask you a few questions about Ms. Parkes."

"Looks like I showed up just in time," Nathan said as he stepped onto the veranda.

"Hey, Nate! How've ya been?" Detective Belafonte reached out to shake Nathan's hand.

"I'm good. What're you doing here, Alex? I thought you were working homicide in Harrisburg."

"I was. Mom got sick. I had to come back home. After she died I stayed…to keep an eye on some stuff going on with Dad."

"Sorry to hear that," Nathan said. He turned to Fiona. "Alex and I went to the academy together."

"Mm."

"Um, how'd ya get past the crime tape, Nate?"

Nathan shot him an ornery grin. "Like Mom always says, if you act like you belong, they'll let you through. It helped that I flashed my badge real quick like. What's going on? Why are you questioning Fiona?"

"How do you know Miss Quinn?"

"Fi's my girl," Nathan told him, as he made his way to Fiona's chair, kissed her on the cheek, then ruffled the hair on Harriet's head. Suddenly wide awake, Harriet's tail wagged madly.

Nathan laid a protective hand on Fiona's shoulder. Her heart swelled at the white-knight-like gesture—but the pet name Fi? Not so much.

"She's being questioned about a murder."

"*Fiona*? She's a kindergarten teacher—no way could she murder anyone."

"I didn't murder anyone, Nathan. I found the body—it was Wyla Parkes," Fiona put in.

"The author that you came here to work for?" Nathan asked.

"Yep. And for your information, being a kindergarten teacher has nothing to do with anything. Don't you remember that librarian who killed her boyfriend several months ago? If a *librarian* could kill someone, why couldn't a kindergarten teacher? I mean, everyone has a temper, don't they? Everyone has a limit, a breaking point, the stick that breaks one's camel's back. I'm no different than anyone else, Nathan. I just happen to be a kindergarten teacher." She leaned back in the chair, crossing her arms over her chest. "I should seriously consider taking that second-grade teaching position that's going to be available soon. I'm qualified for the job, you know. Maybe people would start taking me a bit more seriously—you're always saying things like, *Fiona* couldn't do this or *Fiona* couldn't do that because she's a *kindergarten* teacher. Well, what if I were a *second-grade* teacher? Would I be capable of wicked evil dastardly things then?"

"Really?" Detective Belafonte asked with great interest. He dug into the pocket of his jacket and pulled out a small piece of candy in a red wrapper.

"*No*. Not really," Nathan said, firmly.

Chuckling, Detective Belafonte tossed a small piece of chocolate into his mouth. In turn, Nathan retrieved a bite-size Snickers from his pocket, unwrapped it, and flipped it into his mouth. Locking eyes, the two detectives chewed on their treats.

Seriously? Fiona shook her head. "Okay, look...I spoke to Wyla Parkes earlier in the evening. I dunno, maybe it was around seven o'clock? She came to the cottage to tell me that she'd received the email I sent her with my edits, and to give me a box of chocolate truffles from Belafonte's Bakery. Oh...is that any relation to you, Detective?"

"My dad owns the bakery," he replied, around the mouthful of candy.

"Tony Belafonte is your father? Wyla seemed to be very fond of him. She said he was always bringing her goodies from the shop."

The detective glanced at Nathan and then back to Fiona. "What edits are you talking about?"

"That's why I'm here. I'm editing her manuscripts. I really don't know Wyla very well. She's a friend of my mother's—and there's no way my mother killed her, she's in Daytona, Florida as we speak."

"And you didn't kill her either, right?" Detective Belafonte suggested.

Fiona lifted a shoulder. "Why would I? As I said, I barely knew her."

Taking out his notepad from his jacket, the detective said, "Okay, Miss Quinn. Tell me everything that went on before you found Ms. Parkes's body."

"Well, I'm going to have to begin with what I saw last evening on the beach—"

Fiona went on to tell him about the argument she'd witnessed on the beach the day before, and the spat she'd overheard between Wyla and Lester that morning. She repeated the conversation she'd had with Wyla when she brought the truffles to her door and wrapped the statement up with the woman and dog jogging along the shoreline just before she'd discovered the earrings in the sand and Wyla's body.

The detective meticulously wrote down the information, while Nathan leaned against the same arch where Officer Reeves had been propped, seemingly paying no attention, as he tapped at his cell phone.

"So you're certain that you have no idea who the man or the woman on the beach were?" Nathan asked.

Fiona shrugged. "The man might be this Sam who Wyla's publisher, Lester, mentioned. As for the woman—I have no idea."

Gesturing to the information he'd brought up on his phone while unwrapping another piece of candy, Nathan said, "Lester Crane…he's the head honcho at Noble Publishing—the publishing company Wyla's books are through. Mr. Crane lives in New Jersey, but the publishing company is located in New York City. Wow. He must be really unhappy that she's going independent for him to make a trip from New York to talk with Wyla personally about the book. Just think of all the money he'll be missing out on. But a popular author's last work? Oh yeah, that's *big time* motive."

"This is *my* case, Landry," Detective Belafonte said tersely.

Fiona was a bit taken aback. His tone was a bit too harsh, in her opinion, but Nathan didn't seem the least deterred by his attitude. Tossing another tiny Snickers into his mouth, Nathan said, "Of course it is, Alex. I would never get in the way of a criminal investigation. How long do you think it'll take you to figure this out?"

Keeping a steady eye on his friend, the detective reached into his pocket and pulled out another piece of candy. "How long are you gonna be in town?"

"I have to report to work by six Monday morning." Nathan snorted. "You think you can find the murderer by then?"

"Interested in a friendly competition?"

"A wager?"

"Why not? It'll be like old times—the two of us trying to solve the case before the other." Detective Belafonte pitched the chocolate in his mouth. "Let's see…whoever solves the murder first—by Sunday evening, that is, the other has to buy dinner at Ferrante's Winery. It's located nearby at Geneva on the Lake. Good food, great atmosphere, usually has entertainment, and if you like, great wine too."

"Hm…sounds interesting. Steaks?"

"Mignon."

"Mm, steep. Here's the thing: you've got full access to all the pertinent information from the crime scene," Nathan pointed out.

"And you've got full access to the only real witness—Miss Quinn."

"You mean the only witness that we are aware of—until the jogger on the beach is identified."

"That's true. Are you in or out, Detective Landry?"

A wicked grin formed on Nathan's lips. "Oh, I'm in—I'm way in."

Locking eyes, the two men bumped fists. Detective Belafonte turned to leave and then turned back.

"Before I leave, I want to ask Miss Quinn just one more question." Reaching into his pocket, he tossed a bite-size Kit-Kat onto the wicker table sitting in front of Fiona. He gestured for Nathan to place a piece of his candy on the table too. Nathan obliged. Belafonte asked, "Which is better, Miss Quinn, Snickers or Kit-Kat?"

Fiona's eyes narrowed. Was he serious? They'd just made a wager over a murder case, and now they wanted her to choose between their candy bars? Or was this some kind of murder police trick question? If she chose the Kit-Kat, she was responsible for Wyla's murder? But if she chose the Snickers, she was clear of any suspicion? Maybe it was the other way around. Or was the question fueled by testosterone?

Ridiculous.

Cuddling a sleeping Harriet into her arms, Fiona pushed up from her chair, strolled over to the sliding glass doors, and peered through at the clock hanging on the wall in the small living room. "It is now two-thirty in the morning, gentlemen. I'm exhausted. Am I permitted to remain at the cottage?"

"Yes, Miss Quinn. Since the cottage is not attached to Ms. Parkes's residence, and we've searched it for any evidence, and we've searched your laptop as well, you may stay at the cottage, and you may keep your laptop. Oh, and here's my card. You can contact me twenty-four-seven if you should remember anything else. I always answer my cell—no matter what," Detective Belafonte said.

Fiona took the card and filed it with Officer Reeves's. "Thank you. As far as the chocolate candy is concerned—I'm pleading the fifth. Good night, gentlemen." With that, Fiona went into the cottage, sliding the door closed behind her.

By the time Nathan came into the cottage Fiona had washed up and changed into her soft grey pajama pants and a matching grey cami. Harriet hadn't wasted any time—she was sound asleep smack-dab in the middle of the bed. Fiona placed Officer Reeves and Detective Belafonte's cards in a wristlet she'd brought along for her six-week stay. The wristlet had a lovely hand-painted beach scene on it. She made her way into the living room to find Nathan punching away at his cell phone.

Leaning a shoulder against the wall, Fiona asked, "Aren't you going to bed?"

"In a while. We've got a murder on our hands."

"You mean you've got a wager to win. What happened to we'll spend some time on the beach, go biking, and maybe get a little fishing in?"

When he looked up from his cell, Fiona raised her right eyebrow at him expectantly. Straightening, Nathan said, "No problem. Tomorrow morning we'll rent some bikes and ride over to Belafonte's Bakery on State Street to see what we can find out about Wyla's visit there—when she bought the truffles."

"I never said Wyla *bought* the truffles. I said Wyla *brought* me the truffles. Good night, Nathan." She went into her bedroom and closed the door.

He jumped up from the couch and hurried to her door. Tapping on it lightly, he asked, "Wait a minute—how did she get the truffles? Did someone bring them to her? Tony Belafonte?"

"Good night, Nathan," Fiona called from the other side of the door.

Three

Nathan looked beat. Fiona was fairly sure he hadn't gone to bed until it was almost daylight. She thought she heard his bedroom door close around five-thirty, yet there he was sitting at the kitchen table sipping coffee at seven o'clock. While she cooked breakfast, she was trying to figure what was keeping him upright in the chair. Yesterday he'd worked a full shift doing his murder police job in Pittsburgh, drove three hours to Erie, and then stayed up doing who knows what. He'd said they were going to rent bicycles today—with his droopy eyes and disheveled appearance, she was wondering how he was going to manage the lengthy bike ride he'd planned to State Street and beyond. If nothing else—watching an exhausted homicide detective maneuver a bike should prove to be interesting.

Fiona also noticed the bowl of snack-size Snickers in the middle of the table. There were wrappers lying on the coffee table in the living room and several crumpled up around the bowl in front of him. He'd been hitting the candy hard during the night—maybe it was the chocolate rush that was keeping him from falling face-first into his coffee mug. She sighed to herself. Nathan's little compulsion on Snickers bars was far better than an addiction to alcohol or drugs, she supposed.

"Fi—"

Hm, he'd been calling her 'Fi' every now and then. Fiona hadn't decided if she liked it or not. Problem was, the pet name Fi could possibly transform into Fifi—she was *not* a French Poodle. She would have to decide quickly if she was going to allow the cutesy endearment to continue or nip it in the bud. She was leaning way toward nipping.

Plopping two fried eggs from the pan onto his plate, she said, "You look like a train wreck. Did you ever go to bed last night…or should I say, this morning?"

Dragging his fingers through his hair, Nathan studied the eggs. "Are these over-medium?"

"Yes."

"No salt—just lightly peppered?"

She kissed him on the top of his head. "Just the way you like them, Detective Landry."

"Thank you. I went to bed around six, I think. Did a lot of research on your author friend, Wyla Parkes. Did you know she's published fifty-two novels? And your mom was the editor for the last twenty?"

"She's a very popular romance author, and mom's been editing for her for several years. What else did you find out?"

"I've got Tavia doing some work from the office—mostly on Lester Crane, Wyla's publisher. I also have her working on Wyla's past marriages—all *five* of them."

"Wow. She was married five times? Mom said she'd been through a lot over the years." Fiona's eyes widened as she gasped, "*Mom*! I never called my mother to tell her about Wyla. Oh, this is not going to be pretty. Not pretty at all."

"Maybe not, but she'll be a treasure trove of info—"

As if on cue Fiona's cell phone rang. She grabbed the cell off the kitchen counter. The phone's screen announced, Nancy Quinn. On a braced breath and a roll of her eyes, Fiona answered the call. "Hello—"

"Fiona Nicole!" Her mother wailed into her ear. "Why didn't you call me immediately? I can't believe it! I just saw it on the news—Wyla's been murdered. Poor thing! The news said she drowned. How awful! Are you okay? You weren't there when it happened, were you? Do they know who did this? Do they have any suspects? What does Nate think? I'll tell you what *I* think: they should hang the person who killed her from the highest tree!"

So many questions to dodge. Fiona needed to choose carefully.

"They don't hang people anymore, Mom—well, not in Pennsylvania anyway. Maybe Texas, they seem to have their own set of rules in Texas. I think I read somewhere—"

"*Fiona*! What's going on up there?"

"The investigation has just begun. They are looking to question her publisher, Lester Crane. Do you know a man by the name of Sam who would have a connection to Wyla?"

"No…I don't think so. Wait, Sam Urick?" Mom asked

Fiona laid her cell phone on the table and turned on the speaker so Nathan could hear the conversation. She asked, "What about Sam Urick? What's his connection to Wyla?"

"I don't know much. Wyla was saying that she was considering taking him on as a co-author on the anthology you're editing. All the big time authors are doing such things nowadays. She said Sam hadn't written anything in a very long time. His career had gone totally south and she was hoping to help revive it a bit. But for some reason, I think she changed her mind. I'm fairly sure she wasn't going to sign a contract with Noble Publishing for the work either. I think she was going independent on the anthology." Mom let out a whimper. "Now she won't publish it at all because she's *dead*!" Her whimper turned into weeping. She blew her nose loudly into a tissue. The sound reverberated through the phone like a fog horn.

Fiona winced.

Nathan dropped his chin into his palm, while he slowly stirred his coffee.

"Do you think Lester Crane could harm her—especially since she wasn't going to publish the anthology through his company? That's a lot of lost revenue for Noble," Fiona said.

Nathan nodded while giving her a sleepy thumbs-up signal—she'd obviously asked the right question, and he was awake enough to notice.

Her mother replied, "I don't know. I've met Lester a time or two. He seemed very nice, even tempered, but when you take money away from someone, you never know what they are capable of. I will say that Wyla was worried about telling him that she wasn't publishing Waves of Romance with Noble. Perhaps he isn't as even tempered as he seemed."

Fiona and Nathan exchanged raised-eyebrow glances. Fiona continued her semi-subtle interrogation. "Nathan told me that Wyla had been married five times."

"Oh, yes," Mom let out a fearful gasp. "I wonder if that Harlan Wiggins had anything to do with her death. He was husband number three. He was very handsome and charming, but he was nothing but a blood-sucking gold digger. He was never around when Wyla needed him, and I think he was unfaithful too. To be honest, I think she still gives him money when he needs it. She always had a soft spot for Harlan—the little *weasel*."

"Harrison—Harlan," Fiona murmured to herself.

"What?" Her mother and Nathan asked in unison. Fiona shook her head.

Nathan grabbed the phone from the table and pressed it against his chest so Fiona's mother couldn't hear him whisper, "Ask her if she knows where Sam and Harlan live."

Fiona nodded her understanding. Nathan placed the phone back on the table.

"Fiona…are you still there?"

"Yes, where does Harlan live? Is he in Erie?"

"No, he lives in Pittsburgh. Moon Township, I believe. He was such a little shyster. I never could understand why she couldn't see through his act. Love is blind, I suppose." She let out another whimper.

"How about Sam Urick? Where is he from?"

"I have no idea. I've never met him. Wyla just told me about him when I offered for you to take my place for the editing job." She sniffled. "I think she may have been romantically involved with him at some point, but I can't be sure. Poor Wyla. I'll be coming to Pittsburgh for her funeral, of course."

"Pittsburgh? Won't she buried here in Erie?"

"I doubt it. She was from Pittsburgh. Her family's there. She never had any children, but she has two brothers and several nieces. Oh, Fiona, I can't talk about this anymore. My head's spinning. I've got to take an aspirin and lay down. I'm just thankful that you weren't involved and that you're safe. You'll be going home, I'm guessing."

"Not quite yet. I have some things I want to clear up here. Go lie down, Mom. I'm so sorry about your friend." Fiona disconnected the call and laid the phone on the table.

She looked up to find a svelte smile on Nathan's lips. He said, "You're turning into a very good detective, Fi. You're starting to know all the right questions to ask."

Fiona snatched a Snickers from the bowl, ripped it open, and then popped it into her mouth. Around the mouthful of gooey chocolate, she said, "I hope so."

As exhausted as Nathan had appeared, he was showered shaved and dressed in no time. They drove Fiona's Mini Cooper to Port Erie to rent the bicycles—Fiona got a yellow bike with a darling white basket attached to the handlebar so Harriet would have a place to ride along. Nathan ended up with a blue bike—no basket. Harriet was enjoying the ride. She sat up in the basket with her front paws perched on the rim for the two-mile ride. Her white fur blowing in the light breeze, she'd let out an authoritative bark when they passed someone jogging along the street with a dog or another dog riding in the basket of a passing bike. Fiona kept a close eye on the joggers—particularly the women, but none of the women were jogging with a yellow-ish-brown dog. Perhaps the woman on the beach last evening was strictly a beach jogger. She glanced over her shoulder. Nathan was keeping up well—the four cups of coffee he'd gulped down during breakfast must've kicked in.

Belafonte's Bakery came into view. "We're gonna stop in at Belafonte's," Nathan called out.

"What for?"

"We need some cookies and information."

"Mmmm…more truffles."

Suddenly a police siren sounded from behind them. Nathan and Fiona hit the brakes when they saw Detective Belafonte's cruiser pull up to the curb and park near the bakery.

"I wonder what they want," Nathan said.

Officer Reeves slid out of the cruiser. He wasn't wearing a uniform—he was sporting a pair of jeans, a blue T-shirt, and flip-flops. He approached Nathan, but Detective Belafonte remained inside the cruiser.

"Hey, Nate," Officer Reeves called out, then he nodded at Fiona. "Good morning, Ms. Quinn, how are you today?"

"I'm fine, thanks. Have you found out who the woman on the beach was?"

"Um…I'm afraid not. Do you mind if I borrow Nate for a few minutes? Alex would like to talk with him in the cruiser." He hitched his chin toward the vehicle. Nathan booted the kickstand on the bike to the pavement, then made his way to the vehicle and slid inside the cruiser via the passenger door.

Officer Reeves made his way over to where Fiona was waiting. She asked, "Are you undercover today?"

Looking down at his clothing, he chuckled. "No, I'm off duty. I'm just riding around with Alex. I do that sometimes before my shift. I'm hoping to make detective someday, so I'm trying to learn all I can. He's good—really good."

"Mm."

—⁓—

"What's up, Alex?" Nathan asked once inside the cruiser and the door was closed.

"Talked with Lester Crane—Ms. Parkes' publisher. He's got a solid alibi. He was on an airplane to New York at the time of the murder."

"Mm."

The detective stretched his back and then winced. "Ya know, my back and legs have been buggin' me lately. I've got a really bad cramping going on in my right leg—think I'm gonna have to get out and stretch it a bit. I'm gonna leave the coroner's report for the Wyla Parkes murder on my seat. I'll be back in—oh, three, maybe four minutes."

Nathan leaned way back in the seat. "I'll make sure no one takes it."

"Thanks, buddy."

"You're welcome."

The detective grabbed a file folder from the dashboard and placed it on his seat as his slipped out of the cruiser. He hesitated for a moment and then grabbed a cell phone that was lying on the dashboard.

With narrowed eyes, Nathan watched him shove the phone into his pocket as he walked toward Fiona and Officer Reeves. He glanced at the dashboard clock, eleven a.m. Knowing he had a limited amount of time, he grabbed the file and began to read.

—◦—

"I thought you wanted to talk with Nathan," Fiona said when Detective Belafonte approached.

"I gave him something to chew on. He'll join us in a minute. So…did you enjoy the truffles from my dad's bakery?"

"They were delicious." Fiona gasped. "Oh! I hope we didn't eat evidence."

The detective chuckled. "I think you're good to go." Turning toward Officer Reeves, his tone grew concise when he said, "You left your cell on the dash. You should keep it on your person at all times. This isn't the first time I've had to give it to you, dude." He dug into his pocket and flipped the phone at his comrade.

Officer Reeves blinked back as if he were surprised the phone was not in his own pocket. He reached for the phone only to miss the hand-off. The phone slipped from Alex's hand. Fiona and Officer Reeves grappled for the phone before it fell to the sidewalk, they failed. The phone crashed to the cement.

"Uh, oh, the screen is cracked. No, it's more like smashed," Fiona said, handing it to the officer.

Officer Reeves pressed a few buttons. "It's broken. It won't turn on."

"Sorry. Thought you had quicker reflexes. You'll need to replace it immediately," Alex pointed out. "I'll drive you to the station, you can get your car and go get a new phone. A good detective is never without their phone."

The officer let out a beleaguered breath. "I'll have to stop by my apartment first and change so I'm ready for duty later."

Just then Nathan joined the small group. Detective Belafonte said, "That was quick."

"Got what I needed. Did the phone survive the crash?"

Still pressing buttons and fumbling with the cell phone, Officer Reeves shook his head no.

"We'll be on our way—places to be, people to see. Have a nice day," Alex said.

Nathan and Fiona watched the two men make their way to the cruiser, get inside, and drive away.

"What was that all about?" Fiona asked.

"He let me read the coroner's report."

"That was super generous of him—considering what's at stake or should I say, *steak*?" Nathan chucked. Fiona continued, "So, what was the official cause of death?"

"She was strangled, but that wasn't actually the cause of death. She must've passed out. The killer thought she was dead and pushed her into the lake. Her trachea was crushed. She was either unconscious or didn't have the strength to pull herself out of the water, after all, we're talking about a sixty-two-year-old woman. Anyway, she drowned. Whoever killed your author-friend was angry, very angry. We need to find the man she was arguing with on the beach."

"So we're no longer concerned about the jogger?"

"Why would you say that? We're going to take a nice ride along the street above the beach. Maybe we'll bump into her—or the dog after we go to the bakery of course."

Leaving the bikes behind and with Harriet tucked under Fiona's arm, they strolled toward Belafonte's Bakery. When they arrived at the door, Fiona hesitated. "Um, I'm not sure I should go in. I've got Harriet. They may not approve—"

Just then the door opened and a little old lady with silver-white hair stepped out of the bakery with a tubby blond Pomeranian on a leash.

Nathan quickly grabbed the door to hold it open for the woman who was trying to control the Pom while balancing several bakery boxes tied together with string. The woman nodded and smiled her thanks as she stepped onto the sidewalk to hurry away.

"I think it's okay. C'mon, it smells really good in there," Nathan said.

Wow, he was right. One step inside the door and the enticing aromas of freshly baked pies, cakes, and pastries filled Fiona's nose. The long line of display cases that ran the length of the narrow shop were overflowing with cookies, all kinds of goodies bursting with creams or fruity jellies, and cakes of all sizes and shapes lavishly decorated with colorful icing. Instantly, Harriet's tongue hung out of her mouth. She began to pant—Fiona couldn't blame her.

Fiona followed Nathan's gaze to an older man of about sixty-five or so at the end of the counter carefully placing a tray of cannoli into the display. The man was tall and wispy thin. His hair had more grey with dark streaks than the other way around. His white chef coat hung loosely on his lean body.

"Hey, Mr. Belafonte, Tony, how are you?" Nathan called out.

The old baker looked up. Recognition instantly filled his face. Smiling, he said, "Nathan Landry, how have you been? It's been such a long time."

Making his way toward the man, Nathan extended his hand over the display case to shake Tony's. "It sure has. I've been talking with Alex about the homicide he's working on."

Tony's expression turned sorrowful. "Such a shame. Wyla Parkes was so talented. I've read every one of her books, and she signed a few for me too. She was so beautiful. I admired her so and took her my cookies and cakes all the time. She liked my goodies, and I enjoyed sharing with her." Furtively, he glanced around the shop and lowered his voice. "My wife didn't like it so much."

"Your wife? I'm sorry, I thought Mrs. Belafonte had passed away."

Tony's gaze dropped to the floor. "Oh, yes, my Beverly passed almost two years ago now. I remarried."

"I see. So, you took Ms. Parkes baked goods... *often*?"

"Almost daily."

"And your wife didn't like it?" Nathan tossed Fiona an "imagine that" look.

Tony let out a sigh. "Ah, you know how women can be, jealous. Perhaps I jumped the gun. Perhaps I remarried too soon. I married Tempest a mere nine months after Beverly's passing. I may have married out of loneliness rather than love. Alex warned me. He wasn't happy. I didn't listen." He tossed his hands in the air. "Foolish old men. Never mind me. What can I get you?"

Stepping up behind Nathan, Fiona cleared her throat.

Taking Fiona's cue, Nathan said, "Truffles. I'm told you make incredible truffles."

"Truffles? My truffles were the last goodies I took to Wyla." He shook his head as if he were trying to shake the memory away.

"And that was the last time you saw Ms. Parkes alive?"

"I'm afraid so."

"What time did you take the truffles to her?"

"It wasn't the day she was mur—before she died. It was the day before. I always took them to her on my way home. We close around three and I always take her something that I baked around one, the last round of baking for the day—that way it would be nice and fresh." Pulling the tray of truffles from the case, he said, "You're right. My truffles are incredible, and a dozen for you and the lovely lady—on the house."

Four

"Wyla was right," Fiona said as she placed Harriet back into the basket on her bike.

Nathan draped the plastic bag that held the box of truffles from Belafonte's Bakery over the handlebars of his bicycle. "About what?"

"Well, she mentioned to me that Tony brought her baked goods when she gave me the truffles that day. She said he was handsome, and for an older man, he is. She also said she thought he was interested in her, and she was hopeful that that was the case. She didn't mention a wife—deceased or otherwise. I have a feeling that *he* didn't mention a wife either."

Fiona noticed that Nathan wasn't particularly surprised by what she'd just told him, but without remark, he mounted his bike and pushed off. He was waking up. His lack of sleep the night before was diminishing—pure adrenaline was in the driver's seat now. The investigation was moving forward with a few leads—a good direction to go.

She asked, "Where are we going now?"

"Hope you're up for some serious biking—about six miles to Lakeside Drive."

"That's right back to Wyla's place."

"Tony lives right along there—maybe we'll bump into his new wife, Tempest, strike up a conversation, and see how much she disapproved of Tony and Wyla's relationship."

"I don't think they had an actual relationship."

"Tony thinks they did. Maybe his wife thought so too," Nathan noted.

"Yikes."

The heat was already coming on, so the six-mile peddle back to Lakeside Drive was quite exhausting. Fiona was starting to regret that Nathan kept his obligation to go biking—somehow it simply didn't seem worth the effort. She was dreading the ride back to Port Erie to retrieve her Mini Cooper. What was she thinking when she taunted him this morning with his list of things they could do?

Sweat was pouring from her brow and Harriet's enthusiasm for the ride in the basket had faded by the time they made the turn onto Lakeside Drive. The little dog had curled up in a ball and was sleeping at the bottom of the basket. With her legs starting to tire and her bottom getting sore, Fiona was wishing she could curl up for a nap too—especially after they'd passed Wyla's driveway and continued down the road.

If memory served her correctly, she remembered Wyla telling her that Tony lived approximately one mile down the beach. *Approximately*—she also recalled that Wyla couldn't remember Tony's last name or the name of his bakery. She was hoping that Wyla's sense of distance was better that her memory and Tony's house wasn't any farther than a mile.

Finally, Nathan slowed down and dropped his foot to the pavement. Just ahead a short slight woman was walking toward her mailbox. It appeared that Nathan was stopping to talk with her. Fiona slowed her bike and came to a stop behind him. Harriet was awakened by the jolt. Ears perked, she sat up to peek out of the basket.

"Good morning," Nathan called out to the woman. "We just bought the house at the end of the road."

The woman looked perplexed. Little wonder, there was no house along the road with a for sale sign in the yard. Fiona was trying to figure where he was going with his statement or straight up fib, as it were. Nathan let the kickstand down on his bike and walked toward the woman. Leaving Harriet in the basket, Fiona followed suit.

"Really?" the slim middle-aged looking brunette said. "I didn't know anything was for sale along here. Which house?"

He reached his hand out to shake hers. "I'm Nathan Landry, and you are?"

"Stephanie Friend," she replied, shaking his hand.

"Well, to tell you the truth, Stephanie, I'm a little worried about our decision to move here. I heard there was a murder on the beach last evening."

Stephanie hugged her mail to her chest. Her eyes grew wide. "Oh, how terrible was that? I just can't believe it. We've never had anything like this happen here before. This is a very good neighborhood. Terrifying. Just terrifying. Is this your wife?" she asked, gesturing toward Fiona.

Nathan glanced at Fiona, and then back to the woman. "Um…no…not yet anyway. We're going to move in—"

"We are?" Fiona blurted out. "Who made *that* decision? I thought we were getting married. That's what I told my mother when we bought the house—you know, the one here on Lakeside Drive, or *wherever*."

Both Fiona and Stephanie looked at Nathan expectantly. His jaw worked for a moment, but nothing was coming out. Finally, he managed, "We'll talk about this a little later, Fiona. I'm sure our neighbor doesn't want to hear about our marital status."

Fiona cocked her head to one side. "Are you *sure* she doesn't?"

"Very sure." He turned back to Stephanie. "Anyway, Fiona enjoys jogging and she was looking forward to jogging the beach." Another white lie, but hey, who was she to argue? Nathan continued, "Now I'm not sure it's safe to send her out there. Do you jog? Maybe you could jog together, you know, safety in numbers."

The woman chuckled while waving a handful of mail at him. "Oh, goodness no. I don't do anything that would cause me to sweat. I don't like to sweat, so I don't exercise, and I would certainly never go jogging. I'd melt!"

Just then a beautiful Golden Retriever came bounding around the side of the house. The dog barked at the sight of Harriet in the basket, then the Retriever ran toward the bike to put its paws up on the handlebars knocking the bike to the ground. Harriet leapt from the basket, growling her annoyance at the Retriever who was sniffing at her. The dog's yellow coat and collar shimmered in the sunshine.

Fiona's eyes widened. She met Nathan's gaze and gave him a subtle nod to confirm that she believed this to be the dog she saw with the jogger the night before.

"Patsy! That's not nice!" Stephanie scolded the Retriever as she grabbed the collar to pull her away from Harriet, who was now in full-blown snarling mode showing her itty-bitty teeth.

Fiona scooped Harriet up. "That's such a beautiful dog."

"Now here's your jogger," Stephanie said. "Patsy jogs the beach every evening with Tempest." Her eyes brightened. "There you go—you should talk with Tempest Belafonte. She lives right next door. She jogs the beach every evening with my Patsy. That poor woman who was murdered might still be alive if she walked the beach with a dog. Most people won't bother someone with a dog—they're afraid of getting bit."

Fiona glanced down at Harriet. She wasn't sure she agreed with Mrs. Friend's theory. Harriet was hardly a threat to anyone, but perhaps a bigger dog, like the Golden Retriever, would deter an assailant. Maybe.

"Tempest?" Nathan repeated as he pointed to the house a short distance away. "She lives right there? Do you think she'd like to have a jogging partner?"

Stephanie shrugged. "I'm not sure, but she might. She's not home. I saw her leave the house about fifteen minutes ago. But I'm sure you'll be bumping into her since you're moving into the neighborhood. Just look for Patsy and you'll know its Tempest. She's tall and very thin, pretty, about forty-two or three. She's married to a much older man, Tony Belafonte. He owns a very popular bakery on State Street. His first wife was so sweet, but she died and he married a younger woman right away. I found it to be a bit scandalous, but isn't that the way with men? Anyway, Fiona, you should come over sometime. We'll have coffee and get to know each other—since we're going to be neighbors and all."

"That would be nice. I'd like to meet your husband too," Fiona said, as a UPS truck pulled up.

"My husband?" She cleared her throat and then turned her attention to the delivery truck. "Oh, good, my stuff is here. It was nice meeting you. I'm sure I'll be seeing you around." With that, she made her way up the sidewalk with a good hold on Patsy's collar. The

UPS delivery man followed with two huge boxes on a dolly marked, Island Candle Company.

"That's the dog I saw with the jogger," Fiona said. "And the jogger must've been Tempest Belafonte."

"You're sure?"

"Yes. The dog was wearing a shiny collar and it was a yellow dog—like a Golden Retriever. I'm sure Patsy's the one unless all the dogs on Lakeside Drive are big and yellow and wear shiny collars. How weird would that be?"

"Very weird." Nathan's cell phone rang. He pulled it from his hip pocket. "Landry—" He listened. "What? I know it's all there." He listened while wearing a baleful look. "I don't make those kinds of mistakes." He let out an irritated sigh. "Okay, thanks a lot, Tavia. I'll be in touch." He ended the call and turned to Fiona. "Let's get back to the cottage. I need to throw a bag together. Could you call the bike rental and tell them we'll return the bikes tomorrow and pick up your car."

"Where are you going?"

"To Pittsburgh. The D.A. is claiming that one of the pages from my report on a recent murder is missing. Don't know how that could be, but I've got to get back and take care of the problem. I'm not happy, but while I'm there, I'll take the opportunity to talk with Wyla's third husband, Harlan Wiggins."

"Don't you want me to come too?"

"Actually, no. I want you to take a walk on the beach around the same time you did last night—see if you bump into the current Mrs. Belafonte. Hopefully, she's a creature of habit. I'd like you to strike up a casual conversation and see if she saw or heard anything while she was jogging the evening of Wyla's murder."

"Okay, I can do that, but, aren't you going to tell Alex that the jogger is most likely Tempest?"

They postponed their conversation while the UPS man passed to return to his truck. The driver waved as he drove away.

Nathan continued, "Not just yet. Tempest is his stepmother—a very young attractive stepmom. I want to find out how they get along."

"Oh, by the way, since you're going home, could you please stop by my house? I'm expecting our tickets from Pittsburgh Ballet."

"What tickets?"

"To Swan Lake next month. Don't you remember? You said you'd take me, so I ordered tickets to the ballet. You aren't going to back out, are you? You *promised* you'd go."

"I would never break a promise. I just forgot about it. Of course we'll go."

Fiona noticed Nathan's tentative demeanor as he rubbed the nape of his neck.

"Yeah, sure…I'll stop by your house and see if the tickets have arrived."

"Thank you."

"Fi—"

She sighed quietly. There was that pet name again. She really needed to decide if she was going to let that continue. She searched his face. It was obvious that he was struggling with something. Like he had a question or a request but just couldn't come up with the words.

"Yes, Nathan."

"Um…never mind."

"Are you sure? You seem like you want to ask me something," she pressed.

"No…I'm good."

Still, she had to wonder, did Nathan have regrets about agreeing to take her to the ballet? She was certain she could find someone else to go in his place. Maybe Tavia would enjoy the performance. Or… was he hesitant about going to her house? Which of course made her wonder—what was Evelyn up to? Her grandmother shouldn't harass Nathan, and if she was…wait a minute, Evelyn was her *deceased* grandmother, a ghost, what was she going to do about it if dear ol' dead grandma was playing tricks on her boyfriend? Send her to time-out? She's a spirit for cryin' out loud.

Hokay, maybe she shouldn't have asked Nathan to stop at the house.

Maybe she should retract her request.

"Fiona…are you coming?" Nathan asked, pulling her from her muse. By the look on his face, she could tell he'd been trying to get her attention for several moments.

"Oh, yes. Listen, Nathan, you don't have to stop by the house if you don't want to. I mean, I don't need the tickets right now. I can get them when I go home. I just didn't like the idea of them lying on the foyer floor, but it's not a biggie or anything—"

"No…no, it's fine. I'll stop in and see if the tickets have arrived. You're right, something as important as tickets to the ballet shouldn't be left lying on the floor. I'll go. It's no problem…no problem at all."

Yep. *Something* was going on between Nathan and Evelyn. She didn't even want to imagine what kind of tricks Evelyn was pulling when Nathan stopped by the house. Yikes. Pushing off to start for the cottage, Fiona let out a weary sigh.

Fresh and sassy after a long nap on the veranda, Harriet danced and jumped all around her mistress in anticipation of the walk that was obviously about to happen. Fiona put on her shoes, pulled on a hoodie, stuffed her cell phone in the kangaroo pouch of the hoodie, and grabbed the leash from the hook just inside the door. She glanced up at the clock on the wall.

"Okay, Harriet, we're right on schedule. It is about ten minutes before we left last evening for our walk. We'll either bump right into her or we won't. Let's go." She slid the glass door open. Harriet raced out of the cottage, across the veranda, and onto the sandy beach.

The sun was making its lazy descent over the lake. Crystal waves shimmered in the cast of golden rays, while silver sprays of water leaped into the eventide sky. As she strolled close to the water's edge, Fiona couldn't help but think about the walk she'd taken a mere twenty-four hours ago. The sunset was just as magnificent the night before. The warm breeze sweeping across the lake lifted her hair and tickled her cheeks. Only this evening there were no footprints in the sand—human or canine. It seemed that she and Harriet were the only two wandering along the beach. Perhaps Wyla's murder had deterred Tempest from her twilight run. She couldn't blame her. Fiona was feeling a bit freaked out herself. It wasn't too much farther up the beach where she'd discovered Wyla's—suddenly Harriet's barking changed from playful into a familiar growl. It was a growl she used when she was frightened or felt threatened or there was a stranger at the door.

Fiona scanned the beach. Her heart was beating so hard inside her chest that it felt like fists pounding trying to escape. Harriet barked and growled and snarled at the tide drifting onto the beach and then slipping away. Fiona stopped dead. It was as if her feet couldn't move. She couldn't believe what she was looking at. How could this happen two nights in a row? Sure enough, a woman lay in the tide—face down.

Urgency filled her to her core. She couldn't get away from the beach fast enough. Scooping Harriet up, Fiona ran as fast as she could through the heavy sand toward the closest house which was on the other side of a sand dune. She could see the roof of the house peeking from the other side of the sand swept knoll. Her mind was racing almost as quickly as her feet with a horrifying thought—perhaps Wyla hadn't been murdered by someone who was angry with her. Perhaps she was actually a victim of a serial killer! A serial *beach* murderer! Double yikes!

Five

Patsy sat next to Fiona with her chin resting on her knee. Ignoring the Retriever, Harriet cuddled in her mistress's arms. It seemed the dogs were very aware of Fiona's grief and were silently trying to offer what comfort they could. In the distance, sirens wailed. When Fiona ran toward the houses— any house on Lakeside Drive in search of refuge, she didn't realize it was Stephanie Friend's door she ended up pounding on. Stephanie was more than happy to let her in and called 9-1-1 immediately after Fiona explained what she'd found on the beach—another dead body.

Stephanie's home was elegant. The décor reflected the fact that the house sat on a beach. A white sectional couch filled the room. A beautiful Whiskey Mink full-length coat lay over the ottoman. Grand portraits of ships on stormy waters adorned the walls. Over the white subway brick fireplace was a print of a mermaid kissing a sailor. The house smelled like blueberries. Pillar candles were lit throughout the living room—there were at least a dozen on the hearth, four on the mantle, the coffee table, and end tables held candles—all burning with the sweet scent of blueberries. It was pleasant and overwhelming at the same time.

"Your fiancé won't want to move into the neighborhood for sure now. Or at the very least he won't allow you to jog the beaches. Who could blame him? I may move out of this neighborhood myself. I'm so glad that I didn't come across that Parkes woman's body, or this would be the second time I'd have to dial 9-1-1. They'd begin to think I'm involved or something." Stephanie said as she fumbled to dial the emergency number—it took her three attempts before she finally got her fingers to cooperate. At one point she'd dropped the phone.

"I thought you said you never go to the beach," Fiona said.

"Oh, no, I go to the beach—I just don't jog it."

It wasn't long before the police and ambulances arrived, and once again, Fiona was directed to have a seat and wait, while the police and investigators headed in the direction she sent them.

Through the slight gap in the front curtains, she could see blue and red and bright white lights slicing through the dark. She shuddered. Two women murdered on the same beach in as many days—in a relatively safe community. What was the connection between famous romance author, Wyla Parkes and this woman—whoever she was? If there was no link between them at all, then the situation was direr than originally thought. She hugged Harriet tighter to her chest. She didn't want to even consider the possibility of a serial killer.

Once again, Officer Reeves had been assigned to accompany her until a detective could question her. Unable to see the beach from any of the windows, he stood on the other side of the room watching what little he could through the same gap in the curtains. He was antsy, shifting from one foot to the other, sending a text, checking his cell phone, scowling at his cell phone, dragging his fingers through his hair, leaning against the wall, and then returning to see what he could through the curtains. At one point, he even made a trip to another window to look out toward the Belafonte's house. He wasn't nearly as unsettled when Wyla's body had been discovered. What was that about? Maybe he was annoyed at being left behind with the witness, or whatever Fiona was considered, yet again.

"You must've drawn the short straw again, Officer Reeves?" Fiona asked, in an attempt to make pleasant small talk—anything to quell the thoughts of a maniac killer roaming the beaches of Lake Erie.

He tossed her a lissome smile. "Not at all, Ms. Quinn. You are a very pleasant person to wait with, and I've gotta hand it to ya, you're prime for finding dead bodies."

"Gee, thanks."

He nodded toward the hearth where the candles still burned. "She sure must like blueberries."

"You mean, Mrs. Friend? She must," Fiona agreed.

From the foyer, they heard the front door open and close. They could hear the low murmur of voices in the foyer—a man and a woman's voice. A moment later, Stephanie came into the room balancing a cup in her right hand while slipping her cell phone into the pocket of her skinny jeans. Detective Alex Belafonte followed her into the room. The detective stopped when he came upon Officer Reeves and whispered something to him. The color instantly drained from Officer Reeves' face. He glanced at Stephanie, then made a hasty exit. Alex watched him with narrowed eyes.

What's that about?

"Fiona…Fiona—"

Fiona looked up, realizing that Stephanie had been trying to get her attention. She extended the cup she was carrying toward her. Fiona said, "I'm sorry, I'm a little distracted this evening."

"It's okay. You've had a rough time of it. Detective Belafonte is here to talk with you. I've brought you some tea. I hope you like chamomile, it's supposed to be calming."

"Thank you, Mrs. Friend," Fiona said, taking the cup from her hand.

"Please, call me Stephanie." She glanced at the detective who was looking at all the lit candles.

"Whoa, like candles much?" Alex asked.

"They help me to relax," Stephanie said.

"How is Dr. Friend?"

"Oh, he's out of town. I'm sure he's fine. If you'll excuse me, I'll leave you to talk with Fiona." With that, she turned to leave the room when she noticed the mink lying on the ottoman. "Oh, dear, I'd forgotten I laid you here. I should get you out of the way," Stephanie said, seemingly talking to the mink, as she gathered the gorgeous sable-colored coat up and hurried from the room.

Fiona took a sip of the tea while watching the detective over the rim of the cup. After raking his fingers through his hair and rubbing the nape of his neck, he sank into the overstuffed chair positioned at the end of the couch. He looked tired and a bit distraught, but he managed a meager smile.

Feeling the need to break the ice and get a conversation in gear, Fiona asked, "Stephanie's husband is a doctor?"

"He's a dentist."

"That counts. I kind of feel bad for him—he'll be coming home to a wife who wants to move after two murders in her neighborhood."

"Don't know when he'll be home or if he'll be coming home, for that matter. Dad said that she threw Richard out several days ago. His office has been closed all week. Must be off licking his wounds somewhere—probably at their vacation home in the Outer Banks. Anyway, speaking of murders, you're batting a thousand, Ms. Quinn. Two dead bodies in as many days. You're on fire. By the way, where's Nate?"

"I'm not exactly thrilled to be the one finding the bodies, Detective. It's not like winning the Powerball drawing or anything like that. I'm not going to get a billion dollars or a trip to Italy. I'm going to have to answer a bunch of questions that I really don't have answers for—not to mention how horrible I feel for Wyla and this woman. I can't imagine their fear. On top of it all, I'm starting to feel like Jessica Fletcher."

"Yes, of course. I'm sorry." He chuckled softly. "I'll bet Nate's mom just loves you."

Fiona blinked back and then blinked back again. "What? What's that supposed to mean? You've met Nathan's mother?"

"Um…er…yes, haven't you?"

"I have not. What's up with that? Why hasn't he introduced me to his mother? Am I not the kind of girl that one brings home to one's mother?"

"Seriously? You're a kindergarten teacher."

"Why does everyone constantly refer to that fact? Why does everyone feel compelled to remind me that I'm a kindergarten teacher at every turn?"

Alex's mouth opened and then closed as if he simply could not find the proper reply. He cleared his throat, and then said, "I…I don't know. Could you just tell me what happened and why you were on the beach this evening? After yesterday, I'd think you'd avoid the beach at all costs."

"I was hoping to bump into the jogger from the night before. Not that I would actually recognize the person because, of course, I didn't get a close up look at her. At least I think it was a her—it looked like a woman, it had to be a woman. But I think I would've recognized the dog. Remember, I told you that the jogger was with a dog?" She glanced down at Patsy, who was staring up at her with doggie compassion in her dark eyes. Fiona wasn't sure if she should mention that Patsy was indeed said dog. "Anyway, if I was lucky enough to bump into her—the jogger, I mean, I may have been able to get more information about what happened to Wyla. If the jogger had seen anything, that is. I mean, we don't know for sure that she did. At least that's what I was hoping for. It didn't happen, of course. Unfortunately, I got way more than I bargained for." She sighed. "I really just want to go home."

"We all got more than we bargained for this evening, Ms. Quinn. Do you know the dead woman on the beach?" Alex asked while fumbling with something in his pocket.

"No. If I had known her, wouldn't I have told the first responders her name? Why would you ask me that?"

"Not necessarily. Oftentimes panic turns to shock and pertinent information can be lost at that moment. You knew Ms. Parkes. I thought maybe—"

"I was *working* for Wyla. I didn't really know her. She was an old friend of my mother's—I told you all of that. As for the poor woman on the beach, I have no idea who she is…er…was."

Finally, he retrieved a snack-size Kit-Kat bar from his pocket. As he began to unwrap the candy, he asked, "Kit-Kat?" She shook her head no. He continued, "Okay, are you going to tell me where Nate is?"

"Nate?"

"Yeah, Nathan, your boyfriend—Detective Nathan Landry?"

Fiona's cell phone rang. Thank God. She wasn't sure how she was supposed to answer Alex's question. She retrieved the phone from the kangaroo pouch of her hoodie. The screen announced, Nathan Landry.

Looking up at Alex, she asked, "It's Nathan. May I answer it?"

"Not yet. I need to tell you something first." Alex tossed the Kit-Kat bar into his mouth.

—⁓—

Whatta waste of time, gas, and mileage. When Nathan had arrived at the precinct, Tavia had discovered the missing page to his report. The page was right there the entire time—in the D.A.'s defense, it was stuck to another page. Okay, lesson learned, maybe he shouldn't chew on a Snickers while filling out reports, or at least he should make sure his fingers aren't sticky when handling the pages. At least they got the report and the case could move forward.

The waste of time and energy only continued at the home of Wyla's third ex-husband, Harlan Wiggins. As Nathan pulled up to the driveway, paramedics were loading Mr. Wiggins onto an ambulance—under a white sheet. Mrs. Wiggins was hysterical. The man had suffered a massive heart attack during dinner—right in the middle of eating his mashed potatoes. Needless to say, he never got a chance to question Wyla's third husband. If Harlan had anything to do with Wyla's untimely demise the good Lord was most likely discussing it with him at this moment. Alex claimed that Lester Crane had a solid alibi, so that left Sam Urick unaccounted for—literally. How did Urick figure in—if at all?

Expelling a beleaguered breath, he steered the vehicle onto Oxford Street and rolled to a stop in front of Fiona's house. Sure enough, the porch light was on. He scrubbed his chin with his fingers. He'd picked up the mail on Thursday before he left for Erie, so only today's mail—if there was any, should be in the foyer.

He stepped out of the car.

There should not be three piles of mail on the stairs—only twenty-four hours had passed. Actually, there should've never been three piles of mail on the stairs. He couldn't figure what that was about.

Nathan made his way up the walk.

C'mon, there had to be a perfectly logical explanation for why the porch light was on—even though he was certain that he'd turned it off. Maybe it was on an automatic timer, although he hadn't seen any evidence of that.

He climbed the short set of steps and crossed the porch. He slid the key into the latch and pushed the door open. Coming to a dead stop, Nathan stood in the doorway. There were several pieces of mail on the floor under the mail slot, and catching his eye was an envelope marked, Pittsburgh Ballet Theater propped up on the square newel at the bottom of the staircase—right at eye level. It looked like someone had deliberately placed the envelope there so it would be seen immediately.

Remaining in the doorway, he glanced around the foyer, down the hallway that led to the kitchen, and then he leaned in just a bit so he could see into the living room. The house was still and quiet. No one was about and nothing had been touched—except for the Pittsburgh Ballet envelope. Nathan let out a sigh.

Weird.

Very weird.

Too weird.

He took one step into the foyer, snatched the envelope from the newel, shoved it into his pocket, slapped the light switch for the porch light into the *off* position, and then dashed out of the house, locking the door quickly.

Something was going on in Fiona's house. What? He had no idea, and he wasn't sure he wanted to know. Over the past year that he'd been in a relationship with Fiona, he'd witnessed some strange activity in the house. When he'd question Fi about the weird commotion, she'd clam up tight. Again, he had to wonder if she didn't trust him enough to confide in him because he knew darn well no one else was collecting her mail. As he hurried across the porch, he heard a *click*. He stopped and turned. The porch light had turned on.

"Yeah, okay," he mumbled to himself as he made his way back to his vehicle. He didn't have time to fuss over an obstinate porch light. He needed to get back to Erie as quickly as possible.

His cell phone rang. He fished his cell phone from his pocket, the screen announced, Tavia Andrews. "Hey, Tav, what've ya got on Sam Urick?" He listened, sighed, and then said, "Okay, that's what I was worried about. Thanks."

He disconnected the call and dialed Fiona's number. The phone rang and rang. He was beginning to worry, but right before the voice mail picked up, Fiona answered, "Nathan—"

She sounded out of breath. "Fi, is everything okay?"

"No. Not at all. There's been a second murder on the beach, very close to where Wyla's body was," Fiona explained. Her voice sounded panicked. He felt bad for leaving her behind.

He was afraid that he already knew the answer, but Nathan asked, "Who found the body?"

Fiona's voice cracked when she replied, "I did."

Guilt washed over him. He should've let her drive along to Pittsburgh with him. He felt badly that he'd put her in this position. "Oh, Fi, I'm so sorry. Have they identified the body?"

After dragging in a ragged breath, she said, "It's Tempest Belafonte."

Six

Fiona took another sip of her tea—it was cold. No matter. After Alex had finished questioning her, she had to sit and wait for Officer Reeves to take her back to the cottage. Hm, interesting. She'd just realized that she didn't know Officer Reeves' first name. It seemed they'd spent quite a bit of time together in the past two days and yet she never asked, nor did he offer up his first name. Well, it was time to fix that. She would ask him what his name was on the way back to the cottage.

Glancing around furtively, Stephanie came into the room, and then whispered, "Is Alex gone?"

"Yes. He's gone to find Officer Reeves to escort me home. Honestly, I'm more than willing to walk. The fresh air and the short walk might do me some good."

"Absolutely not. You can't go walking out in the dark—not with a maniac on the loose."

"Is that what you think? There's a maniac on the loose? You don't think the two women could be connected in some way?"

Stephanie looked over her shoulder as she replied, "Maybe."

Fiona assumed she wanted to make sure no one was entering the room to hear what she was about to say.

Seemingly satisfied that no one was about, she slipped onto the sofa next to Fiona. "Well, I don't know all that much about that *Parkes* woman, other than Tempest didn't like her very much. She told me that Parkes was after her husband. I was at her house one day and she had torn up a bunch of books that Parkes had signed for Tony—she was a *romance* author, you know."

"Yes, I heard."

"Anyway, Tempest had torn the pages to shreds and threw them all over the floor." Stephanie glanced up at the doorway again. "I don't know why she cared if he was involved with that author. Tempest was seeing someone on the side herself."

"Really? Who?"

Stephanie drew back as if she'd blurted something out that she shouldn't have. "I...I don't know. But she told me that if Tony could have his little flings, then so could she." She leaned in closer and lowered her voice all the more. "To tell you the truth, I think she was having *flings* from day one of their marriage. I mean, c'mon, Tony is a good twenty-five years older than she was. I liked Tempest, really I did, but let's face it—she married him for the money."

"Did you tell Alex this? Does he know that his stepmother was stepping out on his father?"

Pulling away, while grabbing her chest, Stephanie gasped. "Goodness, no! I couldn't tell him that. Poor Tony and Alex are dealing with a terrible tragedy as it is. That information would just make matters worse, don't you think?"

"I suppose." Fiona looked up at the doorway that Alex had exited through only minutes ago. "He didn't seem all that broken up by his stepmom's untimely passing."

"Well, I don't think Alex was too thrilled that his father married Tempest. It wasn't that he and Tempest didn't get along—I don't think that was the case at all. At least Tempest never mentioned anything like that to me. Frankly, I don't think he would've been happy with any woman Tony picked. Alex loved his mom, and I don't think he believed anyone could replace her. He wasn't wrong. I think Tony moved too quickly. As I said before—isn't that the way with men?" She let out a sigh. "I feel sorry for Tony, and for Tempest, but not so much for the author. She seemed like a hussy to me. She spent a lot of time on the beach…talking to men. I read on the internet that she'd been married something like five times—that's the mark of a woman who can't stay focused on one man. Why, even *my* husband—"

"Ladies…" Alex's voice broke through their conversation.

Stephanie flinched at the interruption. Flushed, she shrunk deeper into the couch. It was obvious she was worried that Alex had overheard what she'd just said. Fiona hoped not, too. Although she wouldn't have been surprised if Alex suspected his stepmother's infidelity. Suddenly she noticed that Alex had brought a police officer with him, not Officer Reeves.

Alex said, "Officer Allen will drive you to the cottage, Ms. Quinn."

"Where's Officer Reeves?" Fiona asked, instantly regretting her candor.

She could see the hesitation on Alex's face. He said, "Officer Reeves is no longer available."

"What do you mean, no longer available?"

"I'm afraid he's been arrested for the murder of Tempest Belafonte."

Fiona heard Stephanie gasp, or was it Stephanie? Was the gasp she'd heard really from her own throat? She couldn't believe what she'd just heard. How was Officer Reeves connected to Tempest? He had been so anxious while the investigators were examining the body and searching the beach for clues. She had assumed he was antsy because he was forced to babysit the witness, instead of being in the middle of the investigation. At no time did she think he would be involved in the murder or that he even knew the victim's identity. She exchanged glances with Stephanie, who raised an eyebrow. Fiona had to wonder—were he and Tempest Belafonte romantically involved? Was Tempest on the receiving end of his text messages? She rotated her gaze to meet Alex's. She could see in his eyes that he was uneasy over the officer's arrest. Was he feeling betrayed by someone he'd considered a friend? How could he not feel betrayed?

How awful.

"Ms. Quinn, Officer Allen will take you back now, and he'll make sure the cottage is secure before he leaves. I need to get to the precinct quickly," Alex said, breaking through her funk.

"Of-of course. I'm sorry for your loss, Alex."

He nodded his gratitude, then gestured for her to follow Officer Allen to his cruiser. Fiona patted Patsy on the head. She felt bad that the dog had lost her jogging partner. She gathered Harriet up, and the officer led her out of the house, to his car, and opened the door for her. As she slipped into the seat and settled Harriet on her lap, Stephanie called from her front door, "Be careful, Fiona! Make sure you lock up tight. I know I will."

The short ride down Lakeside Drive to Wyla Parkes' estate was quick and quiet. Officer Allen insisted that she wait right inside the door while he made a sweep of the cottage to make sure it was safe.

"Everything seems to be fine, Ms. Quinn. Good night," he said as he stepped out the door.

"Officer Allen...how did Officer Reeves know Mrs. Belafonte?"

"I'm not at liberty to discuss an ongoing investigation, Ms. Quinn."

"Of course not, I should know better. I'm sorry."

"No worries. Good night, Ms. Quinn."

"Just one more thing, Officer Allen...what is Officer Reeves' first name?"

"Brian, why?"

"I was just wondering. Thank you for everything, good night." With that, she closed the door and locked it. She watched the officer walk to his cruiser, pull out of the driveway, and drive down Lakeside Drive toward the crime scene. Letting out a careworn sigh, she hoped Nathan would be back soon.

By the time Fiona had showered and slipped into her cozy pajamas, Harriet was sound asleep in the middle of the bed. No matter, she wasn't ready, nor did she think she'd be able to go to sleep before Nathan returned, so she decided to see what was on TV. There was a knock at the door. She peeked out the door to see a man standing on the stoop. She didn't recognize him, and he didn't look like a police officer or any of the investigators she'd seen in the past two days.

Making sure the security chain was in place, she opened the door a small way. "Can I help you?"

"Are you Fiona Quinn?" the man inquired.

"Yes."

"May I come in? I'd like to talk with you about Wyla Parkes."

"Who are you? A reporter?"

"No, I'm Sam Urick."

"And the plot thickens," Fiona murmured under her breath.

"Please, Ms. Quinn. I assure you, I have no intentions of harming you in any way. I feel terrible for what happened to Wyla. Lester Crane told me that the police may be looking for me, and I've been in hiding, but I had nothing to do with Wyla's death."

"If you had nothing to do with Wyla's murder, why don't you go to the police and tell them that?"

"I have my reasons, and I'll tell you what they are. Please, I beg you, let me in so I can explain," the man pleaded.

Fiona bit her lip. "How do you know who I am?"

He smiled. "Wyla told me that her editor's daughter was editing Waves of Romance. She told me you were staying in the cottage, and I read your name in the paper."

He appeared harmless, yet his request went against everything she'd been taught by her parents. Nathan would never approve, and his plea certainly went against what she taught her kindergartners: don't get into a car with a stranger, don't answer the door to a stranger, and never, *never* let a stranger into your house. Yet here she was seriously considering allowing him to come in. Sam Urick—a possible suspect in a murder investigation, or at the very least *a person of interest*. Nathan was probably a good two hours away—plenty of time for Sam the serial killer to do his bidding and dispose of her body. Except, if she sent him packing, he could go back into hiding and never resurface. The information he had, or supposedly had, could be vital to the investigation.

Was she insane?

Had she lost her marbles?

Here she was, Fiona Quinn, the responsible, conservative kindergarten teacher, actually considering letting a potentially dangerous man into the cottage.

She glanced over her shoulder toward the bedroom. Yep, Harriet was still sawing logs in the middle of the bed. Well, so much for Stephanie's theory about being protected by the dog.

"Please, Ms. Quinn, I really need to talk to you," Sam said. His voice becoming more desperate by the moment, and Fiona was feeling bad for him.

It was official.

She was one French fry short of a happy meal—maybe three, because she had her fingers on the security chain, and she was starting to lift it from the latch. How could she face her kindergartners in the fall and preach on "stranger dangers?" She was breaking all the rules. Nathan would be—

Nathan!

Slipping the chain back into the latch, while grabbing her cell phone from the table, she said, "Wait one moment. I'm going to make a phone call—"

"No! Please! Don't call the police, I'll leave. I won't bother you anymore!"

"I'm not calling the police. Well, not really. I'm calling my boyfriend—he's a homicide detective from Pittsburgh, not Erie. I'm going to put him on speaker so he can hear our entire conversation. You have to understand, you're a stranger, and I'm a kindergarten teacher. I mean, even if I were a second grade teacher, and I could be, you know, I'm qualified for the position, I've just never submitted my application for the position that has opened up at our school. Anyway, I would need to do this—for safety reasons. We all teach and preach the concept of stranger danger to our students—it's not just because I'm a kindergarten teacher, so please don't feel the need to remind me of my profession at any time during our meeting. I'm well aware that I am, in fact, a kindergarten teacher. Thank you."

Sam snorted. "I understand *exactly* where you're coming from. I used to be a kindergarten teacher. People used to say things like: how odd, a male kindergarten teacher. Or—you're a *kindergarten* teacher? I didn't know men taught *those* classes. My personal favorite was—I bet those little kids are terrified of you—being a man and all. In reality, I think they viewed me as less than a man because I was a kindergarten teacher, not a history teacher or gym teacher. Yeah, *those* guys got *all* the respect."

"Fi...Fi...are you there? Is everything okay?" Nathan's voice coming from the cell phone snapped her to attention.

She lifted the chain and opened the door. "Yes, I'm here, Nathan. I've called you and put you on speaker because Sam Urick is here."

"At the cottage?"

"Yes, he wants to tell us about his relationship with Wyla."

"Ah, Fi—"

Okay, it was now time to start ignoring Nathan when he called her "Fi". It was not her name and she didn't really care to be called Fi. Decision made—time to make a stand against the cutesy pet name. She turned to Sam. "Please, Mr. Urick, have a seat."

"A week or so ago, Wyla had mentioned that you were doing the editing on Waves of Romance. She was so proud that her editor's daughter was working on the manuscript. She felt her work was in very capable hands," Sam said.

"Oh, how nice."

"Fi—"

Sam sat on the couch. Fiona laid the cell phone on the coffee table. That's when Sam announced, "Well, I guess I should tell you that my name isn't really Sam Urick—that's a pen name."

"I see," Fiona said. "Lots of authors have pen names."

"Fi—"

"Yes, they do, but not for the same reason that I have one, I'm afraid," Sam explained, while wringing his hands in his lap.

"Fi—" Nathan let out a loud sigh. "*Fi-on-a*!"

Good boy. He used the correct name. "Could you *please* stop interrupting, Nathan? Sam is about to tell us why he has a pen name."

"I *know* why he has a pen name!"

"My real name is Sam Ursler. By your boyfriend's reaction, I think he recognizes the name."

Fiona's eyes widened. She was fairly certain her heart skipped five beats. She swallowed back the regret that she was terrified she was about to experience.

Sam continued, "I spent nine years in prison for killing the principal at the elementary school where I was a kindergarten teacher."

Fiona let out a gasp before she could call it back—only this time she was absolutely sure it was her gasp and no one else's. This is exactly what happens when she breaks the rules. She had blatantly disregarded every stranger danger rule in the book, and now she had a convicted murderer sitting in her living room

Double yikes with a French-fry-less happy meal on top!

Fiona swallowed hard. Trying to sound as calm as possible, she asked, "And...and you killed Wyla Parkes?"

"No. That's why I'm here. I wanted you to know that I did not kill Wyla. I was upset with her, yes, but I *did not* kill her."

"Do you mind telling us where you were yesterday afternoon, Mr. Ursler?" Nathan asked.

"I was packing up to go back to Ohio—Lima, Ohio. That's where I'm from. No, I didn't have anyone with me to vouch for my whereabouts. I was alone. But I did not go anywhere near that beach or Wyla—not yesterday, anyway."

Fiona was more than happy to let Nathan ask the questions. She was way too busy cursing herself for allowing this convicted murderer to bamboozle her into letting him in the house.

"Why were you upset with Ms. Parkes?" Nathan asked.

"We'd been seeing each other for about six months. I was falling hard for her, and we had decided to write an anthology together, Waves of Romance. She was going to write the first half, and then I was supposed to write the second. But then out of the blue, she dumped me and decided to go independent on the anthology. She said there was someone else. I would've accepted that. It would've been hard for me to swallow, but I would've gotten over it. It's not like we were married for ten years like my wife and I before she decided to—anyway, then Wyla decided to cut me out of the anthology too. I needed that work. I needed to get back to what I loved to do the most—write. I certainly couldn't go back to teaching—not that I wanted to be a kindergarten teacher." He turned to Fiona. "Frankly, I don't know how you do it."

"Well, I've never killed anyone over it, that's for sure," Fiona said. "May I ask why you killed the principal? Not that there's ever a good excuse for murdering someone, there isn't, but you must've had a reason—of some sort."

"It was the oldest reason on the books—he was having an affair with my wife. She taught second grade at the same school."

"Hokay, now what? Are you going to kill me too?" Fiona asked.

"Of course not. I'm not a *serial* killer. I'm not crazy. I don't go around killing people at will," Sam said, affronted.

"You killed your *boss*."

"Well, yes, but that doesn't really count."

"How do you figure?"

"He was having an affair with my wife."

"Oh! Well! That makes it all better." Fiona glanced toward the bedroom. "Harriet…where are you?" It was a stupid question. She knew exactly where Harriet was—asleep on the bed. Again, so much for Stephanie's dog theory.

"Who's Harriet?" Sam asked as he looked around the cottage.

"My dog. Harriet! Come!" Letting out an agitated sigh, Fiona looked toward the bedroom door—nothing.

"Pfft, some watchdog," he scoffed.

"I'm not joking, she'll be out any moment, and then, well...you don't want to be here, that's for sure."

Sam leaned forward to look in the same direction Fiona was looking. "She seems to be otherwise indisposed."

Fiona rolled her eyes. "Tell me about it. In her defense, she can be quite fierce when she's well rested."

"Okay, I'm really sorry, Ms. Quinn, but I'm going to have to tie you up." He yanked a roll of duct tape from the rear pocket of his jeans. "I'm going to leave, and I can't have you calling the police."

"Are you kidding? Don't you think Nathan will do that? I mean, you can't tie him up."

"I think I have plenty of time to get out of here."

Taking her by the arm, he lugged her toward the tiny kitchen and pulled out a chair from the table.

"Seriously! Harriet! Get out here! Attack!"

Again Sam looked toward the bedroom, waiting for a huge dog to appear growling and showing her teeth.

Nothing.

Fiona let out an exasperated huff before she plopped down in the chair. Sam proceeded to tape her to the chair. Once he had her secured to his satisfaction, he hurried toward the door.

He grabbed the doorknob and then turned back. "Seriously, Miss Quinn, you should *never* ignore the stranger danger rules."

"Yeah, I'll remember that," Fiona replied, concisely.

He stepped outside and quickly pulled the door closed. A nanosecond later a bright light shined on the door, and she heard a man's voice call out, "Stop! Put your hands on your head and drop to your knees."

She thought the voice sounded like Alex's, and then other sounds followed—the sound of feet hurrying across the driveway, and more voices, including Sam's, "I didn't kill Wyla Parkes! I had nothing to do with it."

The reverberation of slamming car doors echoed and engines roared to a start. Red and blue and white lights sliced through the darkness and into the cottage windows. With all the commotion, Harriet came running from the bedroom, barking, growling, and snarling at the door. Finally, Alex stepped through the door and looked down at the larger than life Maltese.

"Whoa, you are one mighty little dog. I'll bet no one messes with you." He looked up to meet Fiona's gaze. "Ms. Quinn, how nice to see you again. Nate called and said you might be a little tied up. So we came over to see what we could do." Fiona tossed him a baleful look. "Officer Reeves has requested to speak with you. I don't know why, but I'm obligated under law to inform you. I'm also obligated to say that you don't have to go if you don't want to."

"Of course I'll go. Could you untie...er...un-tape me first?"

Seven

By the time Fiona was untied, or un-taped as it were, took a quick shower to remove all the sticky stuff from the duct tape, changed into street clothes rather than pajamas, and then went with Alex to the police station, Nathan had arrived in Erie. He was waiting for them at the station. Fiona glanced down at her cell phone. He'd made the trip in two and a half hours. He must've been driving up Route 79 North like a total maniac.

"So nice to see you've arrived alive, Nathan. How fast were you moving?" Fiona asked, with reprimand dripping from her tone.

"I could've taken my good ol' time if you'd obeyed the very basics of *stranger danger* rules," he pointed out.

Fiona let out a defeated breath. He was right, of course.

When Alex reached his desk, his body tensed. He cocked his head to one side and narrowed his eyes. Looking down on the surface of his paper-laden desk, he saw his pens lined up in perfect symmetry according to size and color of ink—all the black pens lay together and then all the blue with one lone red pen a few inches away. His eyes slowly rotated to meet Nathan's

"What's this all about?" he asked, gesturing to the track of pens.

"Oh…your desk is a mess. I can't stand a messy desk. Drives me nuts. Ya can't find anything, but it wouldn't be right for me to touch your desk, that would be downright unprofessional, so I just organized the pens. Nasty habit—I keep my pens organized. My mom says I've got a touch of OCD. I don't know if I agree, but at least your pens are now easy to locate and in order."

Crossing his arms over his chest, Alex stared at him with furrowed brows. Fiona found herself doing the same—Nathan's desk back in Pittsburgh looked like it had been dug out from a mountain of rubble after an earthquake. Pens? She doubted he could find a pen on that desk if his very life depended on it.

"You don't think I know what you're doing? I know you, Nate. I know these little mind games you like to play with perps. I remember seeing you do it. I know what you're about." He picked up an evidence bag containing a cell phone lying a few inches away from the line of pens. "You want me to show you this cell phone. Why didn't you just ask?"

"Got me…I did notice the phone. It's broken and the bag is marked, Brian Reeves," Nathan said.

"Yeah, I didn't have time to check it into evidence yet—I had to go rescue your girl but looks like we've got a solid suspect for the Parkes murder, so that worked out well. Anyway, we've arrested Officer Reeves for the murder of my stepmother, Tempest."

Nathan glanced at Fiona and then back to Alex. "How did that come about?"

"I spend a lot of time with Officer Reeves. He spends a lot of time texting—a woman, an older woman that he's been seeing. I had my suspicions it was Tempest—by the way he described her, where she lived, some of her habits, but he never offered a name—until last week, Tempest Holt. He had no idea she was married—she was using her maiden name. At least I *hope* he didn't realize she was married. Was I surprised that Tempest was seeing other men? Was I surprised that she was being less than honest with her lover? Absolutely not. I saw her for what she was—a blood sucking gold digger. She's forty-two, attractive, fit, let's face it folks, she married my sixty-seven-year-old father for his money. I told him not to get involved with a younger woman, but I think he was so lonely that he was easily charmed by Tempest Holt."

"So how did you come to arrest Officer Reeves? What makes you think he killed your stepmother?"

"He told me that he suspected she was married and he was planning to confront her. He wanted a real relationship—he didn't want someone else's woman. He'd sent a text just before we spotted you and Ms. Quinn biking down State Street this morning. If you remember, his phone"—he held up the phone in the evidence bag—"was broken during our visit. I searched his new phone for the text, but text messages don't carry over to a new phone, so I sent some officers over to AT&T to get his old phone. It took some doing, but the tech guys were able to retrieve the text messages from the old phone." He turned the phone on. He held the phone up for Nathan and Fiona to see when the messages appeared—

> *Tempest, I need to talk to you.*
> *Meet me on the beach at 1:00*

Tempest responded:

> *Is something wrong? I thought we*
> *were meeting on Saturday—usual place.*

Brian texted:

> *I need to see you now. Please Tempest.*

Tempest replied:

> *Sounds serious. I'll be there.*

A shiver ran through Fiona. How odd to be reading a text that was written by a now deceased person. It was almost ghostly.

Nathan pointed to the time the text was sent, 10:57 A.M. He said, "Brian said he was going to the phone store to replace his phone and then stop at his apartment. What time did he start duty?"

"He came in at four o'clock and was on time. He had plenty of time to go to the beach, argue with Tempest, things get out of hand—you know the scenario, we've seen it a million times," Alex said.

"Sure have. What time was he at the phone store?"

"The salesgirl told the officers that I sent over that she'd waited on Brian around two-thirty. There's sand in the shoes he wears for work—yet he was nowhere near Wyla Parkes' body the night before, he was sitting with your girl at the author's cottage. He had to have gotten the sand in his shoes from his meeting with Tempest. I like Brian. He was going to turn into a good cop—eventually. I wish it weren't so damaging, but the evidence is pointing directly at him."

"It seems that way," Nathan said.

Fiona asked, "You said he wanted to see me. What do you think he wants?"

"I have no idea," Alex said, pulling a KitKat bar from his pocket.

"Do you mind if I go into the room with her?" Nathan asked.

"He requested to see Ms. Quinn. I'll have to ask Brian if it's okay, but if he agrees, it's fine by me. I'm going to have a conversation with Sam Ursler while you're visiting with Brian. Time is ticking away, and we still don't have our murder solved, Nate, so let's shake a leg." With that, he tossed the KitKat bar into his mouth. "By the way, Ms. Quinn, have you decided which candy bar you like best? KitKat or Snickers?"

"To be honest, I haven't given it much thought, Detective."

With a wink and a smile, he led Fiona and Nathan toward a back room. He unlocked the door and let them through. The room was small and unwelcoming with a table and two chairs. The room also sported a viewing window. "No one will view your conversation with Brian. This is not an interrogation, but if you could, I would appreciate it if you'd encourage him to seek counsel ASAP. You can wait with her, Nate. If Brian doesn't want you in here, you can leave when I bring him in. There will be an officer in the room at all times for your safety, of course."

"My safety? I don't think Officer Reeves would hurt me," Fiona said.

"Protocol," Alex explained before he closed the door on his way out.

Fiona paced the room while Nathan leaned against the wall with his arms crossed over his chest.

"It's very obvious you're used to these awful little rooms," Fiona remarked.

Nathan snorted. "I'm glad that it's obvious that you are not."

Fiona chuckled. "It's not like I haven't seen one before." Nathan's eyes widened. Fiona smiled. "On TV, silly.

It didn't take long until Alex and another police officer led Brian Reeves into the small interrogation room where Nathan relaxed and Fiona continued pacing.

Brian said, "Thanks for coming, Ms. Quinn, and you too, Detective Landry."

"You're fine with Detective Landry's presence?" Alex inquired.

"No worries," Brian replied.

Fiona took a seat at the table while Brian slid into the chair across from her. Nathan stood next to Fiona, while the police officer stood by the door after Alex exited. Fiona felt the atmosphere in the room was all so official and cold. Surely Brian Reeves was acquainted with the officer standing in the room, as well as the other officers who worked in the station that was now his prison. He'd probably eaten lunch with them, maybe had a beer at the bar with them, met their families, and now he was behind their bars being treated like the criminals he used to track down with his fellow officers. How awful.

"Detective Belafonte said you requested to see me. I can't imagine why. I barely know you, Officer Reeves," Fiona said.

"I'm just Brian Reeves, now. I don't have any family. I was raised in foster homes—lots of foster homes.

I want you to know that I did not kill Tempest. I couldn't kill her. I was in love with her."

"I have you figured for about twenty-eight or so, Brian. Tempest was in her forties—that's quite an age difference," Fiona pointed out.

Appearing to be amused by her statement, Brian shrugged. "What can I say? I've always had a thing for older women. T was thirteen years older than me."

"T?"

Brian snorted. "Yeah…T was my pet name for her. Tempest seemed so long and so proper. I like things to be on a more casual level—at least with my relationships."

Fiona looked at Nathan out of the corner of her eye. "Mm, I see. Anyway, didn't you know that she was married to Mr. Belafonte?"

"No, I didn't. I also thought her name was Tempest Holt—turns out that was her maiden name. Look, Ms. Quinn and Detective Landry, I didn't kill her. I know…as a police officer and you as a detective, we hear that all the time, but I didn't do this."

"You are aware that they have text messages between you and Tempest before her murder, right?" Nathan inquired.

"What are you talking about? I didn't send T a message this morning. What do these texts say?"

"You ask Tempest to meet you on the beach at one o'clock." Nathan took a Snickers from his pocket. He tossed several on the table. "Snickers? They're bite-size, just enough for a quick pick-me-up. Feel free to take one, Brian, and you too, Fi."

Fiona shot him a look.

As usual, Nathan was unaffected by her glances of reprimand.

Brian said, "Um…no thanks. Listen, Detective Landry, I didn't send her a text, and I would've never asked to meet on the beach. I never go to the beach. I hate all that sand—it gets in everything—my clothes, my car, and especially my shoes. I can't stand that and it takes days to get it all out."

"You hate sand and the beach? Wow. We loved to go to the beach when we were kids. We used to bury each other in the sand. Hey, you're right, sand is hard to get out of your trunks. Itchy too. My mom used to make my sister and I vacuum the car when we got home—not to mention the sunburn," Nathan said.

"Yeah…anyway, T and I have our meeting places, but I had no reason to meet up with her this morning, other than just to see her. I was supposed to see her Saturday, and yes, I was planning to confront her about the fact that she was married and hadn't been honest with me, but I had no intention of killing her. And no, our conversation would've never escalated to that point." Scrubbing his fingers across his chin, he let out a frustrated breath. "They haven't shown me

these text messages—nor have they mentioned anything about them. Can you tell me *exactly* what the
text said?"

Nathan rubbed his eyes. As he fumbled with the
wrapper on the Snickers, he said, "*Exactly*? Whew! Let
me think...it said—Tempest...I need to talk to you.
Meet me on the beach at one o'clock—"

"Whoa! Are you sure? Did it *actually* say, *Tempest,
I need to talk to you. Meet me on the beach at one
o'clock?*"

"Yes," Fiona put in. "That's what the text said. I'm
sure of it. Why?"

"I told you, I don't call her Tempest—never. I
always call her T, and especially when texting. Tempest
is way too long to tap out. T is shorter. I'm tellin' ya, I
didn't send that text and I didn't kill T."

Fiona spun in her chair to look up at Nathan. "I
believe him...now what?"

"Brian, you need a lawyer, fast. We need that cell
phone so we can have the texts analyzed," Nathan
explained.

"Analyzed? By who?" Brian asked.

Nathan popped the Snickers into his mouth. "I
know a guy."

Eight

"How does one *analyze* text messages, and who is going to do this?" Fiona asked Nathan as they were getting into his SUV.

"Kent Longshore is a linguistics expert for our department. Not all police departments have such an expert—Erie is one of those departments. Anyway, he was an opera singer for the Pittsburgh Opera years ago but started having problems with these nasty growths on his vocal cords. Nodules, I think he called them—they're like calluses, and they can be career killers for singers. Anyway, he had to give up singing, and he found an interest in linguistics—the study of language. He deciphers notes, letters, emails, and text messages for the department. He's good—real good."

"That's all fascinating, but he's in Pittsburgh. Are you going to ask him to drive all the way up here to look at these text messages? Do we have that kind of time?"

"That's the beautiful part of this scenario—his girlfriend teaches music at Edinboro University, so she lives in Edinboro, which isn't too far from here. Kent spends his weekends at her place, so as long as

Brian can get an attorney quickly and the attorney can quickly demand that they charge Brian for the murder, or return the cell phone, maybe we can get Kent to take a look see at the texts—quickly."

"Mm, that's a lot of quickly-s."

"Sure is, and first thing in the morning we're gonna quickly return the bikes and get your car."

"The rental fee for forty-eight plus hours is gonna be a bear, Nathan."

He sighed. "Don't I know it? By the way, Brian was with you while the investigators were on the beach looking for evidence after Wyla's body was found, correct?"

"Yes, you know he was." Fiona's eyes widened. "Wait a minute. The cuffs of Brian's pants were soaked and his shoes were too. But he wasn't part of the investigation team—he was part of the babysitting team. I wonder how he got his pants and shoes all wet that evening."

"Mm. One does have to wonder."

Fiona suddenly realized that they were not going in the direction of Lakeview Drive. "Where are we off to?"

"My car needs washed and vacuumed. The closest carwash is Niagara on 12th Street."

Fiona looked all around the interior of the SUV. "It looks fine to me. Maybe you should consider cleaning out all the paperwork or whatever that mess is in the backseat, but the floors look fine."

Nathan glanced over his shoulder to the backseat. "What? Clean out my briefcase? I think not."

He pulled into the carwash parking area and went into the small office. It wasn't long before he came out, smiling and carrying a package.

"What's that?" Fiona asked as he slid back into the driver seat.

He held the package up victoriously. "Movie night."

Harriet was thrilled to see her mistress and Nathan when they returned to the cottage. She jumped and danced around their ankles.

"So good to see you so well rested, oh, mighty little dog," Fiona said, wryly.

Within moments of walking through the door, Nathan's phone rang. He snatched the phone from his pocket. "Landry."

"Detective Landry, I'm Harvey Berg. I'm now representing Mr. Reeves. I've put in a call to the prosecutor demanding they either return Mr. Reeves' phone or they file charges immediately. If they file charges, I may have to subpoena the phone. I really don't want to do that. This is highly unusual. We don't usually demand evidence until the client has actually been charged with a crime. Mind filling in the blanks for me, Detective?"

"I'm trying to avoid charges, and if he is charged, I don't want this piece of evidence to go missing. Stick with me on this, Mr. Berg, it'll all come together. As soon as you've got the phone, call me. I'll pick it up and take it to my linguistics man. We'll know within hours if Brian Reeves sent those texts, and if he did, charges will be filed immediately, no doubt," Nathan explained.

"If he didn't, as he claims, will we know who did send the texts?"

"Not for certain, but I'll have some hunches."

"Hunches don't win cases, Detective," Harvey pointed out.

"Like I said, stick with me." Nathan disconnected the call.

"Got any hunches on who killed Wyla? Sam Ursler for example?" Fiona asked.

"I'm glad he's in custody, and he's on my short list of suspects. I think Wyla's murder and Tempest's murder are definitely tied together by two of the most common threads—greed and trepidation. We have to figure out who is the greediest, and make sure to escalate their trepidation."

"How long do you think it will take to get Brian's phone?"

"It's Saturday night. It's going to depend on what the prosecutor's doing and how annoyed he gets by having to deal with the request. He may not get around to it until Monday, in which case, I'll be gone. I'd really like to see this through."

"Sadly, it's not your case, Nathan. You have no real obligation to see it through."

"I know, but I feel badly for Brian Reeves. I feel badly for Tony Belafonte, and like most of the victims in my cases, I've never met Wyla Parkes or Tempest, but they were murdered, and they deserve justice."

"You don't think Alex will see to it that Wyla and his stepmother get the justice they deserve?"

"I hope so, Fi. I truly hope so. Well, I think I'm gonna hit the hay. I'm beat."

"I imagine you are. You were up all night—you and your little friend, Snickers." She nodded toward the scatter of candy wrappers still lying on the coffee table in the tiny living room. Nathan pitched her a sheepish grin and then proceeded to gather the wrappers and dispose of them in the trash. "Thank you," Fiona said.

He kissed her lips and then reached into his back pocket and pulled out an envelope. "I want you to pack up your stuff and go home tomorrow after we pick up your car. There's no reason for you to stay here. If Alex needs to question you any further, he can do it over the phone. Here are the tickets to Swan Lake I got from your house."

"Oh, good, they've arrived. I'm glad."

"Yep, there they were—right on the newel at the bottom of the stairs—like someone had put them there for me to find. Does your porch light always flick back on after it's been turned off?"

Fiona's eyes snapped from the envelope to meet Nathan's stare. His right eyebrow was raised. So

her worries were justified—Evelyn had been playing tricks on the poor guy. "Oh…yes…that switch,
I've always had trouble with it. It doesn't stay in the
off position. You know how old houses are—there's
always something that needs fixing. I go through
sooo many lightbulbs because of it." She let out a
nervous chortle while waving a dismissive hand.
"You'd think someone was turning the light on and
off and on and off and…well, I guess I'll just have to
have an electrician look at that switch. It's just never
been a priority. I guess I put up with it because I'm
used to it. I'll have that ol' switch looked at right
away."

"Yes, you should, especially if you're constantly
having to replace bulbs. Electricians are expensive, but
it'll save you money in the long run."

"Mm."

"Well, just get your stuff pulled together for the
morning. Okay?"

"I suppose."

"I'll take that as a yes." He kissed her again, then
bent down to ruffle Harriet's hair. He opened the
package he'd retrieved from the carwash, took out the
DVD it contained and slipped it into the player next
to the TV. His cell phone rang. Pulling it from his hip
pocket, he answered, "Landry."

"They are still holding Brian Reeves, but you may
retrieve the phone from the evidence room when

you're ready, Detective. I look for Brian to be released by the morning. I really don't think they have enough evidence to hold him much longer than that, and if your linguistics expert can come up with something concrete, I'll have him back on the force before you know it," Harvey Berg said.

"That didn't take very long."

Harvey chuckled. "The prosecutor and I are old fishin' buddies. Maybe I got an immediate call back because he *thought* I was going to invite him out on my new boat. Guess I shouldn't have led him on, but we got what we wanted."

"Hope he wasn't too disappointed. By the way, did they dust the phone for fingerprints?"

"Standard procedure. I'm sure they did."

"Could you have them release that information to me as well?"

"I don't see why not. I'll make the call right away."

"And I'll pick up the phone immediately. Thanks, Mr. Berg." Nathan disconnected the call and instantly began to dial.

"I thought you were going to watch a movie—a movie from the *carwash*," Fiona said.

"Are you kidding me? Time to saddle up, darlin'. I've got a murder to solve and a wager to win," Nathan explained, as he pulled the DVD from the player and almost instantly began to tap at the buttons on his cell phone.

Fiona shook her head as Nathan rushed out the door with the phone to his ear.

—ɯ—

When Nathan arrived at Kent Longshore's weekend condo in Edinboro, Kent was waiting for him on the porch. He was expelling a long thick stream of greyish-blue vapor into the air he'd taken in from his e-cigarette. He smiled when he noticed Nathan coming up the walk.

"Hey, Nate. Thought you had the weekend off. What are you doing working a case? That's just crazy."

"Eh, kind of got caught up in a local murder case, and now I feel that I have to see it through. You know how it is."

"That Wyla Parkes murder in Erie?"

"That would be the one."

"Interesting. Whatcha got for me?" Kent asked, then sucked in another long drag from the vaporizer.

"Those things will kill ya, ya know," Nathan pointed out as he handed the cell phone over.

Kent lifted a careless shoulder. "Eh, they haven't proven it yet. Besides, somethin's gotta getcha." He turned Brian's cell phone over and over in his hands, pulled a screwdriver from his pocket, removed the back, and began to poke and prod around in the guts of the phone. Finally, the phone played a little tune signaling that it was turning on. Smiling, Kent replaced the back onto the phone and then began to scroll down through Brian's history of text messages.

Kent's facial expressions changed from contemplative; to narrowed eyes; to raised eyebrows; furrowed eyebrows, and it wasn't terribly long before his lips curled and he looked up to meet Nathan's gaze. "I'm assuming the last four texts are the ones in question because they definitely were not sent by the same person who usually uses this phone."

"You're sure?"

Kent snorted, as he scrolled through the cell phone's settings. "There's no question. Let me show you how I came to that conclusion, and why it didn't take me very long—" With renewed interest, he continued to work through some settings in Brian's phone. Suddenly, his eyes widened. "Whoa, wait just a minute. I think I may have to retract." His eyes narrowed as he tapped at the phone one more time, and then his mouth tipped upward. "Well, well, look what I found—the man knows his way around technology."

Nine

When Nathan returned to the cottage, Fiona was waiting for him. She was sitting on the couch watching TV with a limp Harriet draped over her lap sound asleep. When the door opened, and Nathan stepped through, Fiona sat straight up in her seat. "Well? What did you find out?"

Quickly, Nathan shoved his phone into his pocket. "Just as we suspected, Brian did not send those texts. Are you all packed and ready to pull out in the morning?"

"Why are you so keen on me leaving?"

"I'm not *keen* on your leaving. I just figured it was time for you to go home. You know, sleep in your own comfy bed, get back to your regular routine—that sort of thing."

"I'm not sure I believe you. I think you think there's going to be trouble, and you want me out of the way."

"That's a possibility. There's always the chance that there will be trouble when working a murder investigation or in this case, a double homicide. Anyway, I just have to get together with Alex, discuss the murders, and then collect my dinner. Um, I'm sure he wouldn't mind if you came too, but it'll all be boring conversation about football and old times at the academy, drinking beer, lots of belching. I'm sure you don't want to stick around for that stuff, do you?"

Fiona winced. "There will probably be more bodily sounds being made than belching—especially with beer and greasy food involved. You're right, I think I'll pass. But tell me, who do you believe the murderer is?"

Nathan cleared his throat. "Like I said, Brian did not send the texts, and after thinking it all through, I think Sam Ursler is probably our man—motive, opportunity, it all makes perfect sense. Okay, so you're set to go. We'll pick up the Cooper first thing in the morning, and I'll see you in Pittsburgh sometime tomorrow night."

Fiona furrowed her brows. She could see Nathan was hiding something, though not doing a very good job of it, and she wasn't sure he believed in the Sam Ursler theory. What could she do? Yes, she had packed her things. Would she leave in the morning as Nathan wanted her to?

Hmm.

She wasn't exactly sure.

—⟋⟍—

Throughout her stay, the nights had been dark and quiet at the cottage. Only the sound of the lake lapping against the shore and songs from insomniac crickets filtered through the windows. Fiona loved the sounds of the lake at night—they were different than the sounds from home. At home one would hear cars going up and down Oxford Street at all hours, or the sound of a siren off in the distance—most likely echoes from the Parkway.

Regardless of the solitude that Lake Erie or the restless crickets offered up, Fiona tossed in her bed all night. Her mind was in overdrive. Over and over again the vision of Wyla and Sam Urick/Ursler arguing on the beach played on repeat. As she recalled, Sam appeared more upset than angry—more pleading than demanding.

Rolling over onto her right side for the hundredth time, she checked the time while reaching for the nightstand drawer, it was four o'clock. Trying to sleep was becoming an exercise in not happening. Okay, why not have a little early morning treat? She pulled out one of the Three Musketeer bars she had hidden in the drawer, unwrapped it, and began to nibble.

After fluffing the pillow and flipping onto her back, Fiona closed her eyes while letting the chocolate melt on her tongue. In her mind's eye, she could see the two of them, Wyla and Sam, on the beach in the purple hue of dusk. *Wyla was waving her arms in the air at him, while Sam shook his head. The wind off the lake blew Wyla's wide-brimmed hat from her head as she turned to stomp through the sand back toward the house. Sam hurried to retrieve the hat before it was swept into the water.*

Although Fiona heard almost none of their conversation, she remembered hearing Sam call to the author, *"Wyla, wait! Please, Wyla—we can make this work if you'll just hear me out!" But she didn't acknowledge his cries at all, as they drew closer to the house.*

Fiona remembered hurrying into the cottage and sliding the door closed. She didn't want Wyla or Sam to know that she'd seen or heard anything. She now regretted that decision.

No…things were simply not adding up—not for her anyway. There was no doubt in her mind—Sam was more frustrated with Wyla than cross. Yes, Sam killed a man—out of rage, out of jealousy, and betrayal, but that was a totally different set of circumstances. He'd told Fiona and Nathan that Wyla had broken off their relationship possibly for another man, and he seemed to respect her decision—most likely because she was being honest with him—unlike his former wife and his former, now deceased, boss.

Raking her fingers through her bed-tossed hair, Fiona opened her eyes.

Lester Crane, Wyla's publisher, had the most to lose. His publishing company stood to lose thousands because Wyla had decided to publish Waves of

Romance independently. However, Nathan said Mr. Crane had a solid alibi.

Hm.

Wyla had been married five times.

From what Stephanie had told her, some of the women who lived along Lakeside Drive felt threatened by Wyla's presence. Interesting…were all the husbands in the neighborhood that easy to lead astray?

So was Wyla Parkes the drama queen or femme fatale Fiona had suspected her to be from the very beginning? She certainly looked the part two days ago on the beach, and the characters in her books, like Abigail Wentworth, played the role convincingly.

Write what you know—isn't that the "rule of thumb" for authors?

In any case, could it be that Wyla's murderer was already dead?

Did the jogger, Tempest Belafonte, feel compromised enough by Wyla's relationship with her husband to kill her in order to protect the financial benefits she intended to reap from Tony Belafonte?

Good question.

Indeed they were all good questions, and she knew that Nathan had to be asking himself the same ones—there was no way that he was arbitrarily accepting the Sam Ursler theory—he was too smart, too savvy a detective to be taken in by such a convenient scenario. No, something was up, and that's why he wanted her to go home to Pittsburgh. Just hours ago he told her that he wanted to see this case through. Well, in truth, Fiona did too.

"Fiona...Fiona...c'mon Sleeping Beauty, time to get up. I let you sleep in, but we've got to get a move on this morning," Nathan's voice jerked Fiona from a deep sleep, along with the fact that Harriet was licking her face.

Pushing the Maltese aside, Fiona sat up to find Nathan standing at her bedroom door, dressed and ready to go. She asked, "What time is it?"

"Nine. What's that on your face? Is that...*chocolate?*"

Almost in a panic, Fiona wiped her mouth. No wonder Harriet was licking her face. Yikes, where had she stashed the wrapper from the Three Musketeers bar she'd eaten in the wee hours of the morning? She blurted out, "No...no, I'm sure it's a dust bunny or—"

Nathan snorted. "Are you one of those sleepwalkers who eat while they're wandering around? Have you been in my bag of Snickers?"

Thank goodness. The wrapper from the Three Musketeers bar was under her derriere. She feigned an affronted expression. "I don't sleepwalk, and if I did, I don't think I'd waste my time on a Snickers bar."

"What kind of a candy bar would you go for? Please don't say KitKat—I'd be mortally wounded."

Licking her lips to make sure all the chocolate was gone, Fiona insisted, "This is a silly conversation. Now get out of my room so I can get ready. Is there any coffee?"

"It's made and waiting for you in your travel mug."

Fiona swung her legs out of the bed while pulling the blankets up to make sure the candy wrapper remained hidden. "Great. Thanks. I'll be ready in just a few minutes."

Hurrying through the process, Fiona had the bed made up, did her hair, makeup, got dressed, and was rolling her suitcase into the living room within fifteen minutes. Not bad. Nathan jumped up from a kitchen chair to grab his duffle bag and Fiona's travel mug.

"Perfect, here's your coffee, let's get moving."

"Good thing I'm not hungry."

"Probably because you ate all those Snickers bars."

Fiona tossed him a baleful look. "Pfft—not."

Nathan chuckled.

With Harriett on a leash, they made their way out of the house. The bicycles were secured to the back of Nathan's SUV with several bungie cords. Fiona locked the door, then hesitated, while looking down at the key in her hand. "I'm not sure what to do with the key to the cottage. I mean, with Wyla gone—I mean, deceased, who do I return the key to? I can't just leave it under the mat. Should I hold on to it and give it to a family member at the funeral? And if I did, how would I know which family member to give it to? These things can become very sticky after a death, you know."

"Tell me about it. When my Aunt Stella passed there was all kinds of kicking and screaming over her collection of handcuffs," Nathan said, as he turned to walk toward his SUV.

"Her *what*?"

"Handcuffs. You know, handcuffs—shackles; bonds; fetters; restraints, those things I place on criminal's wrists when they're taken into custody."

She was almost afraid to ask, but she simply couldn't help herself. "Okay…I'll bite…why did your Aunt Stella have a collection of…*handcuffs*?"

Nathan slid into the driver's seat. "Don't know, and I don't think I want to know. But I've seen the collection and it's quite extensive. She had a set of cuffs that were rumored to have been on Al Capone's wrists. Pretty cool—at least I thought so."

After slipping into the passenger seat, Fiona buckled her seatbelt. "So, who finally won custody of the pretty cool collection of handcuffs?"

He started the SUV and pushed the gearshift into reverse. "My mom, of course."

Fiona rolled her eyes. "Why am I not surprised? You mean, your mom, the mom that I've never met? The infamous Mrs. Landry?"

"Do you want to meet her?" he asked as he backed out of the driveway.

"It would be nice. I mean, I thought we were in a relationship. Shouldn't your mom meet the woman you're in a *relationship* with? You've met my family, and c'mon, crazy never takes a vacation when they're around, so don't you think it's high time I meet… what's your mom's name? Good Lord, I just realized that I don't even know her first name."

"Her name is Rita. I'd love for you to meet her, but she's in Australia right now."

"Really? Australia? Last month she was in Belgium."

"She gets around."

"With her handcuffs? Honestly, Nathan, I'm beginning to believe she doesn't really exist. I'm beginning to believe she's a phantom like my grand—" Fiona clamped her mouth closed.

"Like who?"

"Um…er…you know, phantoms; ghosts; spirits; apparitions; dead people who still roam the Earth."

"Like who?"

Fiona managed a nonchalant shrug. "Don't know."

"You do."

"Nope."

"Do so."

She set her gaze on the road before them, so she wouldn't have to look him in the face when she said, "I'm a kindergarten teacher, Nathan. Remember? We are above reproach—incapable of doing underhanded things—like lie."

Rolling his eyes, Nathan let out a beleaguered sigh. "Okay, I created that monster."

"Yes, you did."

Thankfully, the parking lot for the bike rental company was just ahead. Though Nathan appeared completely convinced that she knew a phantom personally, he seemed to be willing to let the subject...die.

Fiona was now certain Evelyn had been up to some kind of ghostly mischief when Nathan dropped by the house. Yikes.

Grumbling under his breath, Nathan paid the exorbitant bike rental fee, and within a few minutes, they were transferring Fiona's stuff from Nathan's SUV to her Mini Cooper.

"Now what?" Fiona asked as he held the driver's side door open for her.

"Now you go home, and I'll see you later tonight."

Fiona placed Harriet inside the car. The little white dog scurried across the center console and sat in the passenger seat, placing her tiny paws on the dashboard—the co-pilot position. Fiona asked, "I mean, what are you going to do right now?"

"I'm going to call Alex, have him meet me somewhere so we can discuss the case."

"Because you truly believe Sam Ursler to be Wyla Parkes' murderer?"

"That's right, and if it wasn't for the fact that I called Alex when Ursler showed up at the cottage, we wouldn't have him in custody right now."

"And now you can collect your steak dinner."

"That's right. But it'll be lunch rather than dinner." He reached over and kissed her. "Okay, time for you to be on your way. You don't want to get caught up in all that Pittsburgh traffic." Fiona slipped into the car and let the window down. "Drive safely. I'll call you when I'm on my way back to the Burgh."

"Hey, you never got to watch your movie."

He smiled. "Oh, I watched it all right. Be careful, Fi, I'll see you soon."

With a quick reluctant nod, Fiona put the Cooper in reverse and pulled out of the parking spot. Yeah, he was in way too big of a hurry to get rid of her. Something was up.

Ten

Fiona hadn't driven very far when she decided to pull off and grab a cup of coffee and think things through. What things? Well, she needed to decide if she was actually going to drive home or turn around. She pulled into the Brick House Coffee Shop on 26th, put Harriet on her leash, and walked up onto the porch of the big brown brick house turned restaurant. The porch had tables and chairs and lights strung from a massive black awning. Other than the awning, the setting reminded her of the porch on her own big brown brick house on Oxford Street. She settled into a chair and dialed Nathan's cell. After a number of rings, the call went to voice mail. Fiona disconnected without leaving a message. It wasn't long until a waitress came out to take her order, and not long after that that she returned with Fiona's latte and a biscuit for Harriet.

Fiona sipped the latte.

Hm, Nathan had supposedly settled on Wyla's murderer—but what about Tempest?

Fiona tapped her fingers on the table while watching Harriet chew the biscuit.

Why would Nathan suddenly dismiss Tempest Belafonte's murder?

Did he believe Sam Ursler killed Tempest too?

Not likely.

Why would he? Sam had no real connection to Tempest unless she had witnessed the murder, and Sam knew that she had. But there was no real evidence to support that theory, nor had Nathan ever suggested such a scenario. Okay, maybe Sam did kill Wyla—a big maybe, but not Tempest, so who killed the young attractive Mrs. Belafonte?

Seriously, it was not in Nathan's demeanor to dismiss a murder, to leave it be, unsolved, and raw.

After taking another sip of the latte, she picked up her cell and dialed Nathan's phone again.

Again, he didn't answer.

Hm.

Wait a minute. She was a kindergarten teacher—not a detective, not a policeman, not an investigator, or a member of the homicide department. This was Nathan's profession. He knew what he was doing, and she needed to step aside and let him do whatever he was planning to do—even if she was feeling uneasy about it. During their relationship, they'd talked about boundaries—especially when Fiona's mother came to town—yeesh. What Nathan needed for her to do was to respect those very boundaries, get in her car, and drive to Pittsburgh, and that was exactly what she was going to do.

Yep.

Uh, huh.

Well…

———ᴀ———

Out of the corner of his eye, Alex noticed that Brian was paying very close attention to his phone conversation with Nathan. Officer Allen kept busy at his desk while glancing in Alex's direction, and then covertly in Brian's.

Brian had been released from custody late last evening and had been permitted to return to work—on desk duty until everything was completely sorted out. Alex lowered his voice only slightly as he told Nathan of a backroad where he used to meet snitches. If one wasn't familiar with the area, it would be very easy to get lost, so he had Nathan write down the GPS coordinates as well. He explained the road was fairly remote and no one should be around to overhear their conversation.

After he made sure Nathan had a handle on where he was going, Alex disconnected the call. When he looked up, Brian's eyes snapped back to his computer screen. Yeah, he was paying way too much attention—the little rat. After exchanging glances with Officer Allen, Alex took in a braced breath, then made his way out of the precinct.

It was go time.

The warm summer breeze whipped through the Mini Cooper as Fiona drove down the interstate toward Pittsburgh. Harriet poked her head out the gap Fiona had left in the passenger side window. She sniffed the air and genuinely enjoyed the wind ruffling her ears and fur. In general, Harriet rarely slept during a road trip—until it dragged on for several hours, and then the little dog would grow weary and curl up on the seat to nap. Gauging Harriet's enthusiasm, it appeared she would be awake for the duration of the trip home. Perhaps she could sense that they were heading for home and was ready to be back in the big drafty house on Oxford Street. Fiona couldn't blame her, she was missing home too. She was hoping that the weeds in her flower beds hadn't taken over too badly.

Still...

She had to wonder if Brian Reeves had been released from police custody this morning as Harvey Berg had said he would be, and did they permit him to return to his place on the police force or would he have to take some time off? Perhaps he'd have to work a desk job for a week or so—it seemed to her that's what usually happened when a police officer got in trouble—at least that's what the news usually reported.

Well…Nathan would tell her what happened with Brian when he called later in the day. And with that thought planted in her head, she tried to focus on the music filtering from the radio—until another thought seeped into mind, *I never had the chance to say goodbye to Alex.*

Hm.

It was official—she was becoming her mother. Yep, if Nancy Quinn found herself in a similar situation, she would totally find a reason to call her boyfriend's old police buddy to glean any information she felt she needed or desired. Fiona never thought she'd take on her mother's persona—guess that ship just sailed. Yeesh.

Fiona knew if she called Alex to tell him goodbye and how much she enjoyed meeting him, she could slip in a question about Brian, and then she wouldn't have to wait for Nathan's phone call—she'd be satisfied because she already had the info, right?

Even though her mother's DNA pumping through her veins was urging her forward, she wasn't sure calling Alex was a good idea.

Still…

Using the Bluetooth in her car, she dialed up Detective Belafonte. His phone rang and rang and rang until it finally went to voicemail. Fiona disconnected the call. Hm. She tapped her fingers on the steering wheel. She contemplated, and then dialed the number again. The detective's phone rang and rang and rang, and again it went to voicemail.

Strange.

She was almost certain that he'd made the comment that a good detective is never away from his phone. The night of Wyla's murder he'd made a point to tell her, "I always answer my cell—no matter what."

As a matter of fact, yesterday while they were talking in front of Belafonte's Bakery, Alex made the statement to Brian, "A good detective is never without their phone."

Yesterday was coming back to her on a rush of memories. *She and Nathan were peddling their rented bikes toward Belafonte's Bakery when Alex's cruiser pulled up to the curb. Brian got out of the cruiser to summon Nathan.*

Fiona's brows furrowed.

After a few minutes, Nathan went to the cruiser, and Alex let him read the coroner's report on Wyla's death. But Alex was left alone in the cruiser for at least three or four minutes alone with Brian's cell phone.

Fiona focused on the exit sign just ahead—Edinboro was one mile away.

Tony Belafonte owned a very lucrative bakery. He married a much younger woman—a woman who very well may have become the beneficiary of Tony's estate.

Motive.

Fiona steered the Mini Cooper onto the Edinboro exit ramp.

After Alex left Nathan in the cruiser to read the report, he walked up to Brian and tossed his cell phone at him—the cell phone he'd forgotten in the cruiser. He didn't hand Brian the cell—he tossed it, on purpose, as if he didn't want Brian to catch it, rather, he wanted the cell to fall to the pavement and break. Now Fiona understood why—because Brian wouldn't know that he had texted Tempest to meet him on the beach!

After making a left turn, Fiona drove down the ramp to return to the interstate toward Erie.

She remembered that Alex insisted Brian should replace his cell phone immediately, but Brian needed to return to his apartment to change clothes first, during which time he would be without a cell phone— Tempest would not be able to contact him. Alex was going to drop Brian off at his car at the station so he could go to his apartment and then to the phone store. Where did Alex go after he dropped Brian at his car?

Opportunity.

Fiona pressed the accelerator down. She was certain Nathan had this all figured out and that's why he wanted her to go home—so she wouldn't be caught up in any of the backlash.

Had Nathan decided to confront Alex?

Where were they going to meet?

Nathan hadn't said, but she had a feeling it was in a clandestine location. That could turn out badly—especially if Alex figured that Nathan was on to him. Then again, she was sure that Nathan was prepared for the worst. Although he wasn't in the habit of carrying heat—he depended on his wits, and his wits may not be enough to get him out of this situation.

Her stomach was starting to tighten into wicked little knots. All of the pieces were coming together, except for Wyla's murder. Why would Alex kill Wyla? Maybe Sam Ursler did kill Wyla after all. No… there was still something missing—a clue she was overlooking.

She started to reach for the Bluetooth when her phone rang. She pressed the button. "Hello…"

"Ms. Quinn, it's Brian Reeves—"

"Brian! I'm so glad you called."

"I wanted you to know that I've been released, and I've been placed on desk duty for a few days until this mess is straightened out."

"I'm so glad to hear that. Do you know where Alex is?"

"Not presently. He just walked out of the station."

"Well, in that case, I'm afraid the mess has only gotten worse. I need your help right away."

—⟋⟍—

After Brian listened carefully to Fiona's theory, he whispered to her, "I think I know exactly where they're going. I'll text you the info. Don't worry, I'll make it work, and I'll get back to you with a strategy." With that, he disconnected the call. He turned to Officer Allen. "We've got a situation. Meet me in the captain's office ASAP."

"Yeah, sure," Officer Allen said. He pulled his cell from his pocket.

"What are you doing? I said we need to talk to the captain."

"I'll be right in, dude."

Eleven

Nathan's GPS led him down a dusty road that wound through a sprawling vineyard. The grapevines hung like sinewy dark skeletons on the wires strung from post to post. The rows of grapes seemed endless, stretching for as far as the eye could see, and then the road dropped over a steep hill into a wooded area. He knew that Alex worked the drug unit for a short time before switching to homicide, and he could see how snitches would feel comfortable meeting a detective in this abandoned area. He hadn't seen a vehicle or a person for at least three or four miles.

As he steered the SUV around a tight bend, Alex's cruiser came into view parked alongside the road. Alex was leaning against the vehicle with his arms crossed over his chest, and his right ankle crossed over his left. His body language was casual, but Nathan knew there would be nothing casual about this meeting.

He slowed the SUV to a stop behind the cruiser, turned off the engine, and then got out to make his way toward Alex, who didn't move a muscle. He remained in his relaxed stance, but his eyes watched Nathan's every step.

"Hope that winery is close by. I can practically taste that filet mignon from here," Nathan said, when he reached Alex's side. He leaned a shoulder against the driver's door of the cruiser to try and match Alex's nonchalant manner.

Alex snorted. "It's not terribly far from here. I guess I do owe you, I mean, you did *basically* bring Sam Ursler in." He glanced over to Nathan's SUV. "You and Ms. Quinn…and she's not with you, right?"

"No, I sent Fi—"

Right then a blue and white Mini Cooper rounded the bend. Dust and gravel spit into the air as the Cooper approached at a pretty good clip. Taken aback—not in a pleasant way, Nathan raked his fingers through his hair. What was Fiona doing there? There was a very strong chance the situation was going to get dicey—he wanted her out of harm's way. Obviously, Fiona had other plans—as per usual.

"Isn't that Ms. Quinn?" Alex asked, gesturing toward the Cooper now rolling to a stop behind Nathan's SUV.

Nathan let out a fraught sigh. "Yep. That would be Fiona."

Fiona stepped away from her car, waving her hand over her head as if she were standing on the deck of an ocean liner waving bon voyage to a zealous crowd on the dock. She hurried toward them, grinning.

Slightly out of breath, she managed, "Nathan, Alex, I just got a call from Brian Reeves. He's been released from custody. Isn't that great? Well, he's been placed on desk duty until this whole mess with Tempest has been cleared up, but he's confident that he'll be vindicated very soon. I knew he didn't have anything to do with her death, didn't you, Alex? I mean, I spent quite a bit of time with him over the past several days. You know, he seemed to always be in charge of babysitting me when Wyla was murdered, and then when poor Tempest was—well, when I came across her on the beach—dead. He's just too nice to have had anything to do with killing Tempest. Don't you agree, Alex?"

"He's a good man—"

"I think so too. I can't imagine him doing such a thing. Sooo, are you two ready to go to lunch? Now? Right now?"

"Fi…I thought you were supposed to drive home… to *Pittsburgh*," Nathan put in, stiffly.

"Oh, yes, I was, and I was on my way when…poor Harriet got sick. She was throwing up out the passenger window. She just kept vomiting and vomiting all down the side of the car. It was terrible. I couldn't drive for two and a half hours with her barfing like that. Whatta mess! I mean, what was I supposed to do? So, I turned around, took her back to the cottage, cleaned out the car, and then I thought I'd catch up with the two of you for lunch."

"And you knew to find us on this secluded back road…how?" Alex asked.

Fiona's eyes grew wide. She had that clichéd "deer in the headlights look" about her. She stuttered, "Nathan told me where you were meeting. Isn't that right, Nathan?"

Nathan and Alex exchanged looks, and then Alex said, "That's really interesting because Nate had no idea where he was going. I know he had to use his GPS to find this place. I helped him with the coordinates. That brings me to you, Nate. If you've got something to say, go ahead, just say it."

The right side of Nathan's mouth kicked upward. "Ya know, my mom really liked you, Alex. She thought you had all kinds of potential."

"Yeah, I know. Rita showed me her handcuff collection. Pretty cool stuff."

"Really, Nathan? He's not only met your mother, but he's seen *Rita's* cool handcuff collection?" Fiona groused.

"The cuffs that Al Capone wore are the coolest of the bunch," Alex said.

"*Rumored* to have worn," Nathan corrected.

"Well, it's no *rumor* that I've never met *Rita* or laid eyes on any of the handcuffs. I've only learned her first name mere hours ago, for cryin' out loud," Fiona put in.

"Nate is under the assumption that he'll be slapping those very cuffs on me, isn't that right, Nate?"

"What makes you say that, Alex?"

"Because you think you've got it all figured out. You think you've got Wyla Parkes and Tempest's murders all wrapped up in a pretty little box, and maybe you do, but there's one problem—I'm not in a co-operating kind of mood."

"I can see that. I wish you'd reconsider, I was really looking forward to dinner. Can I ask what made you snap? Was Tempest flaunting the fact that she had your dad right where she wanted him, or were you just running damage control?"

"Flaunting was not Tempest's style—she was way too cool a customer for that. No, that little witch was as silent as a snake crawling through tall grass. I knew what was going on by my dad's remarks—she was gonna get everything if I didn't step in. What tipped you off?"

"The text message you sent on Brian Reeves' phone and the fingerprints."

"Fingerprints? What fingerprints?"

Lifting a shoulder, Nathan said, "The fingerprints we found on Brian's phone."

Alex blinked back. "You've got my fingerprints on his phone?" He snorted. "Seriously? That's your evidence? Here's a news flash for ya, *Detective*—my fingerprints are all over Brian's phone. Why? Because I was always handing it to him. He was always laying it down and leaving it behind, in the cruiser, on a table in a restaurant, on his desk at the precinct. I've even used his phone a time or two when my phone's battery was low." He tossed his head back in mock laughter. "You found my fingerprints on Brian's phone—that's a good one, Nate!"

"That all makes perfect sense, really it does, except we weren't looking for your fingerprints, Alex. We were looking for Fiona's, and there they were."

Alex's eyes widened, then his brows furrowed. "*Fiona's*? What's Fiona's fingerprints got to do with anything?"

"There were four sets of prints or partial prints on Brian's phone—Brian's, Tempest Belafonte's, yours, and Fi's. But Fi's fingerprints put a timeline on the phone's location. The text in question was sent to your stepmother at 10:47a.m. At that time you were sitting in the cruiser waiting for me to join you so you could share the content of the coroner's report on Wyla Parkes' death with me. Meanwhile, Brian was standing on the sidewalk informing me that you wanted to see me in the cruiser. Brian had forgotten the cell on the dashboard, and you were alone in the cruiser with his cell phone."

"What are you babbling about? How do you know he didn't send the texts *before* he got out of the cruiser?"

"Because when you got out and left me alone with the coroner's report it was exactly eleven o'clock. Don't ask me why, it's probably the detective in me—that

OCD my mom accuses me of having, but I checked the time, and it was eleven o'clock. You made sure you grabbed his cell phone and took it with you. I don't believe Brian could have gotten out of the cruiser, walked down the sidewalk, and had an entire conversation with Fi and me in three minutes, but I do believe it was plenty of time for you to send a text from his phone to Tempest. I couldn't figure out why you had Brian come to get me instead of just walking down the sidewalk with him, and then taking me back to the cruiser. But then I realized it was because you had a plan and needed time to send the text. Brian was nowhere near the cruiser or his phone for at least three or so minutes—that would be during the time the text was sent. Fi touched the cell while you and Brian were standing on the sidewalk waiting for me. I saw the phone fall and Fi pick it up when I was returning from the car after reading the coroner's report. I believe you took the phone and threw it at Brian with the purpose of breaking it, so he wouldn't know you'd sent the text. You were also aware that old text messages would not show up on a new phone, so when Brian got his new phone, he would still be unaware of the text that had been sent to Tempest."

"I'm sorry, Nate, but you can't prove that I sent those texts to Tempest."

Nathan said, "Texts? How did you know there were more than one? I said, a text, you've been using the plural form. That tells me that you know there was more than one text sent."

Alex blew out a frustrated breath. "Text or texts—it doesn't matter, you can't prove I sent them!"

Nathan shrugged. "Maybe I can't, but my linguistics expert can. You see, everyone uses different words or phrases or abbreviations when they speak and especially when they text. Some people will write out a word like, *you*, while others will use the letter "U" to replace the three letters, Y-O-U. Brian is one of those people. Furthermore, Brian never texted or called Tempest by her full name. He would refer to her as "T," even when he was talking to her in person, he called her "T." In the text messages that you sent to Mrs. Belafonte, you wrote words out that Brian would not have, and you typed out Tempest's full name. You also suggested that they meet on the beach—Brian hates the beach, he and Mrs. Belafonte never met or walked on the beach, they would meet at a little restaurant in North East, PA."

"Circumstantial, Nate. It's all circumstantial. It proves nothing."

"It proves that you didn't do your homework before sending that text. I'm surprised at you, Alex. I thought you were more thorough than that." Nathan moved his hand toward his pocket.

Alex reached behind and pulled a gun from the waistband of his slacks and pointed it at Nathan. "Stop! What are you doing?"

"Oh…sorry, I was just getting a Snickers out of my pocket. I need a snack. I thought we were going to dinner, but now I'm thinkin' we might not be. Need one? I know you like a little chocolate pick-me-up too."

Alex winced. "Snickers? No way."

Nathan turned to Fiona. "Snickers?"

"I'm good, thanks."

Turning back to Alex, Nathan said, "I get it, really I do— I understand why you'd do away with Tempest. She was a threat to your future inheritance. If she could convince your father to make her the beneficiary of his money, you'd be out. But why Wyla Parkes? Were you covering all the bases? I suppose you were thinking if your dad dumped Tempest for Wyla, what would stop him from making her the beneficiary? He was crazy about her, and she was another threat, so you killed her too. But here's the thing—you killed her for no reason. Wyla was wealthy in her own right—she didn't need your father's money."

"Sorry, old buddy, you didn't solve *that* murder because I didn't kill Ms. Parkes. I didn't even know that dad was stopping by to give her baked goods or that he had a crush on her until the night of her murder, and Ms. Quinn told me about it. That said, I believe we've got her murderer in custody, at least that's what I intend to prove over the coming days. You lost the bet—big time. I feel bad that Ms. Quinn has to pay too."

Nathan stepped in front of Fiona. "Surely we can come to some kind of an understanding, let's find a way to spare Fi—"

"Okay, you can stop calling me that now," Fiona hissed.

Surprised, Nathan turned. "What?"

"I want you to stop calling me that," Fiona repeated indignantly.

"You mean, Fi?"

"*Exactly*."

"Don't you like my pet name for you?"

"I do not. I don't mind Fi—really I don't. But before you know it, Fi will turn into Fifi. I'm not a poodle, Nathan. Pet names are nice—if you're...*sixteen*. But they tend to get out of control. There was a little boy in my class last year who called his little girlfriend *poopylumps*. Now, what's that all about? Does his father call his mother poopylumps? How awful would that be? Could you pass the sugar, poopylumps? Or how was your day at the office, poopylumps? He's seriously calling the woman a pile of poop...with lumps! I realize that Fifi wouldn't be nearly as bad as poopylumps, but still, I don't want anyone thinking you're calling your dog when you say something like—Fifi come here, please, or Fifi where are you? I'm just sayin'."

"Why didn't you tell me?"

"I'm telling you now. I don't like Fifi and I *certainly* don't like poopylumps."

"You picked *now* to tell me that you don't like Fi?"

"I've never been known to have the best timing, Nathan. *You're* the detective, I can't believe you haven't figured that out by now."

While keeping the gun trained on them both, Alex piped in, "I don't understand what the problem is. I haven't heard him call you Fifi once, and I can't believe he'd ever come up with poopylumps—although, I kinda like that, it has a bit of a ring to it...*poopylumps*. What do you think, Nate?"

Nathan shrugged. "I'm not totally against poopy-lumps. As a matter of fact, I'm kinda sorry that I didn't come up with it. Those kids say the darndest things, don't they?"

Crossing her arms over her chest, Fiona let out a frustrated *harrumph*. "*Seriously*? You've betrayed everyone, Alex. Your father, Tempest, Brian Reeves, and Nathan. You're holding a gun on your old chum for crying out loud, and yet you're sticking up for him? Isn't that just like a man?" As if someone had just slapped her, Fiona's spine straightened, her eyes widened, and her mouth dropped open. "O-M-G! I think I know who killed Wyla, and it's *not* Alex or Sam Ursler."

"What are you talking about, Fiona?" Nathan asked.

"Yes, Alex and Sam had plenty of motive and prob-ably plenty of opportunity to kill Wyla, but neither of them did—but I think I know who did." She smiled at Nathan. "And thanks for calling me Fiona. I like my own name better than any pet name."

Nathan followed Alex's glance toward the wooded area, and then their eyes met.

Alex quickly raised the gun to take aim. "Hey! It doesn't matter what she thinks or thinks she knows. I'm sorry, Nate, and you too, Ms. Quinn, but I've got no choice—"

"Put the gun down, Detective Belafonte!" A loud voice boomed through a megaphone. "We've got you surrounded! Put the gun down and drop to your knees!" Alex didn't move. He locked eyes with Nathan once again. "C'mon, Alex, don't make us shoot. We don't want that. Drop the gun."

Nathan leaned close to Fiona. "Is that Brian Reeves' voice?"

"Sure is."

Nathan exchanged intense stares with Alex as he dropped the gun and fell to his knees, and then he muttered, "Okay."

Police hurried from the bushes to surround Alex. Officer Allen pressed him to the ground to slap cuffs on his wrists while another officer gathered his gun. Brian rushed over to Nathan and Fiona.

"Are you two okay?" he asked.

"We are, thanks to you, Brian." She grabbed Nathan's hand. "But we've got to go. I've got an idea about something."

"I need a statement—"

Fiona called over her shoulder, "You'll get one!"

"Where are we going, and who are we going to see?" Nathan asked while he watched Officer Allen whisper to Alex as he escorted him toward a cruiser slowly rolling down the hill toward the scene.

"I'll explain in the car, c'mon, we've got to hurry."

Nathan pulled her back. "*Fiona*…how did you know where Alex and I were?"

She sighed. "Brian had an idea. He said Alex used to meet informants there. So he put together a sting and sent me in as bait. It worked rather well."

"You think so?"

"Of course, now let's get going before our suspect is long gone. We'll come back for my car later."

Twelve

Nathan rolled his SUV to a stop in front of Stephanie Friend's beach house on Lakeside Drive. He turned to meet Fiona's gaze. "Well, here we are. Are you sure about this?"

"I believe so," Fiona said.

"Okay, I'll give you a shot at your theory. How do you want to play this?" he asked as he thumbed a text message on his phone.

"We'll go in together. I'll keep the conversation light. Who are you texting?"

"A friend—no pun intended." Nathan opened his car door. "This should be interesting."

They walked up the sidewalk hand in hand. The closer they got to the front door the vivid scent of blueberries filled the air. "What's that smell?" Nathan asked.

"Blueberries. Stephanie must love blueberry candles. She has them burning all through the house, although I didn't realize the scent was strong enough to smell it from outside. Maybe she didn't have quite as many burning last night—after I found Tempest's body. How odd. It's a little strong, but at least it's pleasant—or somewhat pleasant." Fiona knocked on the door. Patsy barked. They could hear her toenails tap against the hardwood floors inside. They waited, but no one came to the door.

Nathan peered into one of the long arched windows. Sure enough, dozens of pillar candles flickered throughout the large living room. Fiona knocked again, and still, no one responded. After a few minutes, Fiona tried the door to find that it was not locked. She shot Nathan a questioning glance. He shrugged.

She opened the door and called in, "Stephanie! Are you home? It's me, Fiona Quinn."

"Oh! I'm sorry, I didn't hear the door. I'm upstairs, come in sweetie," Stephanie yelled.

They stepped inside the door. The aroma of blueberries was stronger—almost overpowering. Fiona gestured for Nathan to wait downstairs while she went upstairs to talk with Stephanie.

He whispered, "I'm only giving you five minutes, and then I'm coming up. If you get into trouble, yell."

Fiona gave him the thumbs up signal as she ascended the white staircase with curvy oak railings. Nathan browsed around the large open room. Multiple candles burned in every corner, on every table, the hearth, window sills, and the mantle. Patsy followed behind him as he made his way around, looking at the paintings on the walls and the flicker of each flame.

He coughed.

When he came to the coffee table at the far end of the couch, he licked his thumb and doused the flame from a candle. He looked to a coffee table across the room to find a short stack of coasters. He went over and retrieved one, then placed the coaster over the candles to smother the flames of the two candles on the small table. He glanced down at Patsy, she wagged her tail.

"Hey, Patsy, what's up with all the candles? No one likes any scent *that* much."

The upstairs of the Friend household was as elegant as the downstairs—still carrying on the ocean theme throughout. There were glittery starfish on the walls and a print of a mother and her small children frolicking on the beach. The wide hallway was lined with small tables. Each table had a lit pillar candle on it. The heady fragrance of blueberries drifted through the second floor. Fiona could hear movement coming from the room at the end of the hallway so she headed in that direction. At the end of the hallway under a tall window that looked out over Lake Erie, was a box marked, Island Candle Company. The box top was open. Fiona peered inside—the box contained one unused candle that had toppled over on its side.

"How odd that she would burn so many candles," Fiona murmured to herself.

She found Stephanie in a spacious bedroom wearing the mink coat. Fiona recognized the gorgeous coat from the night before—it had been laying over the ottoman in the living room. The closet doors were open, clothing was strewn over chairs and the bed. Two large suitcases that were half-filled lay on the bed, while smaller cases stuffed with makeup and jewelry sat on the vanity.

Stephanie turned, under the mink coat she was wearing a white sundress, a diamond necklace, and matching diamond earrings that dangled into the fur collar of the coat. Her manicured feet were bare, while at least ten pairs of shoes cluttered the floor.

"Stephanie...what are you doing? And why are you wearing that coat? It's like eighty degrees up here, especially with all these candles burning," Fiona said, unable to stop her brows from furrowing.

"Oh!" Stephanie exclaimed as she twirled in a circle, showing off the mink. "Do you like it? I call her, Vanessa. Vanessa Owens was the woman who Richard had an affair with before Wyla Parkes. And the necklace? Kate Handers, one of his patients, he had an affair with her before Vanessa—that was about two years ago, so I got the necklace. The earrings were given last Christmas, I never did find out who he was fooling around with then, but they're nice. I never asked him for diamonds or a mink. I would've preferred a faithful husband, but isn't that the way with men?"

"I…I don't know, and I certainly hope that I never find out."

"Oh, Fiona, sweetie, I hope you don't either. But let me clue you in—the bigger the gift, the bigger the sin they are trying to apologize for. Took me years to put two and two together, but now *you* know what to watch out for. You're way ahead of the curve. Your husband-to-be *seems* very nice, but you never know. By the way, where's your ring?"

"My…my ring?"

"Your engagement ring, silly. Where is it? I'd love to see it."

Fiona looked down at the naked ring finger on her left hand. She cleared her throat. "Oh…that ring… it…um, was a little too big. It would flip around on my finger, so Nathan took it to the jeweler to have it fitted for me."

"Awe, he does seem sweet." With that, Stephanie returned to her chore of packing clothes into the cases.

Fiona swallowed hard. "Yeah…that he is." She had to find the nerve to ask the pertinent questions she'd come to ask. "So, where are you going? On a vacation? Or did you already find another house to move into, I mean, in light of the recent murders in the neighborhood?"

Stephanie paused for a moment. Fiona could see she was measuring her reply. Stephanie said, "I'm sure the house will be on the market very soon. I certainly don't want to live here anymore. Patsy and I are going to the vacation home down south, and then I may take a trip to France—it's very nice this time of year." She reached for a silk blouse and, with shaking hands, attempted to fold it.

"I see. Will your husband be joining you? I feel bad that Nathan and I never had an opportunity to meet Dr. Friend."

Obviously distracted, Stephanie rumpled the blouse into a ball and pitched it into the suitcase, and then snatched several other articles of clothing and tossed them in on top. "No. I've had quite enough of Richard's shenanigans. He won't be joining me anywhere ever again." She paused, looking up at the ornate crystal chandelier dangling over her bed. "Hm, I have to wonder though, if he'd been given the opportunity, what would've he given to make up for his *fling* with that *Parkes woman?*"

Fiona was working hard to keep her emotions in check. "I *totally* understand where you're coming from. I bet you wanted to kill Wyla Parkes yourself. I know I would've. No woman should mess with another woman's man and not end up in dire straits."

Slowly, Stephanie turned around. "You do understand. Tempest did too. She was in total agreement when I told her what I had planned. I'm not big on exercise, but I did take a self-defense course once. It came in very handy when I took that woman out. I think I may have even crushed her trachea. Tempest was even considering helping. I told her I could handle Wyla Parkes myself. Although, she and her boyfriend went down to the beach to make sure Wyla was dead."

Fiona had to catch her breath. Her thoughts immediately rushed back to the night Wyla was murdered. Brian's shoes were soaked. The bottom of his slacks were wet too, and yet he had not been allowed at the murder scene—he was sent to babysit her on the veranda. Trying to keep her voice level, she managed, "Her...*boyfriend*? Tempest Belafonte's *boyfriend* went down to the beach?"

Stephanie stopped. Her eyes searched the bedroom as if she needed to correct her last statement. "Um, well, yes, at least he *was* her boyfriend at the time. Anyway...I can't believe Tempest's gone. She was a good friend. A confidante." She stepped closer to Fiona. Fiona had the urge to step backward, but she held her ground. "You seem like you would be a good friend too. Trustworthy. If you want to know the truth, I think Alex felt threatened by Tempest. Not physically, mind you, financially. Tempest had Tony under her thumb. I believe he would've left everything to her—she and her then boyfriend were counting on it, I think."

"You…you don't think that Tempest loved Tony?"

Stephanie laughed. "Oh! Goodness, no! Tempest was a blood-sucking gold digger, but she was very nice. Like I said, I liked her, she was a good friend, and good friends are very hard to find these days." She pointed a warning finger at Fiona. "So are good husbands. Too bad you can't show me your ring. Oh, I hope it's not terribly big."

Fiona had to work hard to control the shiver in her words. "Um…I wish I could be your friend, Stephanie. I'll need a friend. I don't know anyone in this community, and actually my ring...it's pretty darn big. I'm starting to worry a little. It's too bad you're leaving. Besides…your secret is safe with me." She moved in closer to Stephanie. "By the way, I know a secret too."

"What would that be?"

Feigning trepidation, Fiona looked over her shoulder toward the bedroom door. She lowered her voice. "They have a man in custody for Wyla Parkes murder. I think the charges will stick. He's been in that sort of trouble before. I mean…he's murdered a woman before—his own wife."

Blowing out a relieved breath, Stephanie plopped down on the bed. "*Really*? Maybe I don't have to leave after all." Her gaze dropped to the floor as if she were searching for her next sentence. "Do you really want to take Tempest's place? If what you say is true—they have a solid suspect for Parkes' murder, then I'll be able to remain here. But I'll need some assistance from a good friend to help me resolve one more little issue."

Fiona feared she was about to get in over her head. "W-what *little* issue?"

—◇—

Finally, Nathan smothered the last candle's flame. Standing in the middle of the vast gourmet kitchen, he looked down at his cell phone. Fiona had been upstairs with Stephanie well over the five-minute deadline. He hadn't heard any kind of a struggle nor had Fiona called out to him for help. He listened—no sounds of distress. Now that the candles had been stifled, the scent of blueberries quickly dissipated and a familiar odor began to rise. Patsy sat next to the basement door, whimpering.

"Something smells fishy, and I think you know exactly what it is, Patsy." Nathan made his way toward the dog. Taking in a big breath and holding it, he opened the basement door. A long dark stairwell lay before him. He felt the wall for the light switch. Patsy bolted down the stairs ahead of him. He could hear her paws thumping against the wooden steps until he found the switch and lit the stairs just as she arrived at the bottom. Patsy waited for him. Dancing in place, her whimper grew in intensity.

The basement area was just that—an unfinished underground room used for storage of unwanted items that the Friend's had deemed not quite ready for the Goodwill or the garbage. The area was dark and dank as most basements tend to be. Shadows scattered throughout the space, and although he needed more light, at least Nathan could see where he was going from the illumination of the staircase. Christmas decorations, Halloween and fall decorations, boxes, an antique sewing machine equipped with a peddle, an old analog TV, and more random boxes piled three and four high were just some of the things put away and forgotten in the underground room. Patsy followed him through the throng of junk.

As much as he dreaded it, Nathan knew he was going to have to follow his nose. He was running out of air anyway, so he let out the breath he'd been holding and breathed normally, taking in the stench he suspected he would experience. Looking around, he noticed a wooden cross buck door that perhaps led to a root cellar or maybe even a wine cellar. He grabbed the handle and yanked, but the door didn't budge. He examined the wall and the door to see if he'd missed a lock, but there wasn't so much as a latch—only the long metal handle. He pulled again, and again, the door wouldn't open. He figured the wooden door frame might be warped or perhaps the door itself had swollen in the dampness of the basement.

Patsy fussed—walking in a small distressed circle.

Nathan placed his foot against the block wall, grabbed the handle with both hands and yanked with all his might. The door bowed and cracked, until finally it flung open, knocking Nathan back against a pile of boxes. The boxes crashed to the floor and over the top of Nathan. Letting out a yelp, Patsy jumped aside.

Nathan climbed out from under the boxes. Letting out a grunt, he winced, while covering his nose and mouth with his hand. He peered into the room—there lie a corpse. "Just what I thought—I've hit the trifecta, Patsy."

Thirteen

Fiona followed Stephanie down the staircase. They had barely reached the halfway point when a horrific stench assaulted them. Grabbing the railing, Stephanie peered down to the living room.

Stephanie let out a gasp, and then exclaimed, "What happened to all of my candles? Who blew out my candles?"

Covering her nose, Fiona was absolutely certain that Stephanie's "*little issue*" was stinking up the house. She was also certain as to who'd put out the candles and there was no doubt he'd discovered Stephanie's little issue as well. Question was—where was Nathan now?

Almost tripping and falling, Stephanie rushed down the stairs. The long mink coat trailed over the stairs, bouncing and bobbing like a long furry tail on each step as she descended. "Hurry, Fiona! Someone's in the house! Patsy! Patsy! Where is that dog? She's much too friendly. I swear she'd probably offer a robber a beer along with my jewelry!" she groused loudly, as she reached the main floor to run across the living room. Vanessa, the mink, slapped against one of the end tables as Stephanie passed, knocking several candles over. *Plunk, plunk.* Deep blue wax dribbled from the freshly doused candles over the surface of the table and onto the wood floor.

Fiona hesitated momentarily at the waxy mess, and almost set the candles upright, but instead continued to track behind her new bestie until she caught up with her at the basement door which was standing open.

Peering down the stairwell, Stephanie whispered over her shoulder, "Whoever they are, they're in the basement. The light is on. This is not good. Not good at all."

Wincing at the vile smell, Fiona covered her nose and mouth. She coughed. Her words were muffled as she spoke through her hands. "Should we call the police?"

Even through the heavy coat, Fiona could see Stephanie's body stiffen. "No! No, we can't call the police!" She grabbed Fiona by the arm. Fiona gasped at the smell as her hand was yanked away from her face—not that her hands were doing all that much to squelch the stink. Stephanie insisted, "You have to help me get rid of whoever is down there, and then you have to help me get rid of Richard's body!"

"*Richard*...you mean, Dr. Friend—your *husband*, Dr. *Richard* Friend?"

Digging her manicured fingernails deeper into Fiona's arm, Stephanie started to drag her down the basement steps. "You said you wanted to be my friend. Well, I need your help to get rid of Richard's body. Surely you understand, I just couldn't take it anymore. He just wouldn't behave himself. I had to put a stop to it all. So I poured just a little bit of peanut oil in his evening martini." They were halfway down the stairs. She paused to explain while sweeping an errant strand of hair from her eyes. "He was terribly allergic. I thought he'd have a reaction within moments, but hours later he was still sitting there—reading the newspaper. Can you imagine? The waiting was practically killing me. He didn't have a reaction until the middle of the night—delayed anaphylaxis, that's what they called it on the internet."

"That's all very fascinating, Stephanie, but—"

"Stephie!" a man's voice bellowed from above them.

Stephanie looked up. Fiona whirled around to find Brian Reeves filling the doorway at the top of the stairs. His cheeks were red with agitation. "Why would you let her into the house? Why would you bring her down here? I told you I'd help you get rid of the body when things settled down!" His icy glare shifted to Fiona. "Where's Landry? There's no way you're here and he's not."

Gagging and coughing, Fiona managed, "Seriously, can't we move this conversation upstairs or outside? Outside would be great."

"We're fine right here," Brian insisted.

"I don't understand, Brian. What's going on? Were you at the beach after Wyla's murder? How are you connected to all this?"

"I told you, I like older women—and they tend to like me. Isn't that right, Stephie?"

Through watering eyes, Fiona glanced at Stephanie, who was gazing at Brian while grinning like a love-struck teenager. Yanking her arm from Stephanie's grip, she turned back to Brian. "But...I thought you were involved with Tempest or *T*, as you liked to call her."

"I was. She and I planned to grow old on Tony Belafonte's fortune. We had his accident all planned out for next week. We had no idea Wyla had her sights set for Richard, and Stephie finally decided she wasn't having it anymore—so she took care of business. She wasn't sure Wyla was dead, so she called T, and we went to the beach to make sure. We were supposed to get rid of the body, but you came up the beach. My T was many things—an adulteress, a gold digger, and she was almost willing to be murderess too. But after seeing Wyla lying dead in the sand? Not so much. She couldn't do it—murder was just going too far—whether it was Wyla Parkes or Tony Belafonte. She decided to wait for the old guy to die of natural causes—that could've taken forever. He was pretty healthy. Anyway, she suddenly had a surge of integrity. Whatta bunch of hooey!

She wanted to report Stephie to the police. She was losing it and neither Stephie nor I could talk sense to her. She decided to end our relationship, possibly come clean about our plans to do away with her husband, and that's when I decided I wasn't having it. I had to do something to protect myself and Stephie, of course. So I'm afraid that's when I had to take care of business."

"You killed Tempest because she didn't want to be part of *two* murders and didn't want to be with you anymore?"

Brian shrugged. "It happens. Sometimes things just don't work out as you planned, and that's when you have to make adjustments."

"*Adjustments*? You consider murder an adjustment? I don't think you have a thing for older women, Brian. I think you have a thing for older wealthy women, and obviously, you're willing to do whatever it takes to get to their wealth—including making…adjustments!" Fiona turned to Stephanie. "I thought you said Tempest was your *good friend*."

Petting the collar of her mink, Stephanie let out a sigh. "Well, guess she wasn't as good of a friend as I originally thought. Poor thing, she had a change of heart or conscience or whatever."

Rapt in complete bafflement, Fiona asked, "And so you took her boyfriend, and then you killed your husband?"

"Oh, goodness no, Richard had already been dead for a day or so. That's why I bought all those candles."

Overcome by the stench of death, not to mention the vile story unraveling before her, Fiona leaned against the railing. "So…you killed Wyla, and Brian killed Tempest?" Brian nodded. Fiona's jaw dropped. "I had the whole thing spectacularly wrong! Poor Alex! We set him up."

"I know, it worked great, didn't it?"

"No! It did not work great—an innocent man was arrested. I still don't understand…the text message… who sent the text messages?"

"Pfft. I've got an app for that. You can pre-schedule your tweets, some Facebook posts, and your text messages. C'mon, Ms. Quinn, I know you spend a lot of time with kindergarten kids, but you've got to get with the times. I also changed my messages to make it look like someone else had sent them, like Alex, for example. I thought your detective boyfriend was sharp— but he didn't figure it out. He's subpar at best." He pulled a gun and trained it on Fiona. "Now…speaking of Nathan Landry, where is he?"

Fiona backed down one step. "I have no idea. He was here. I guess he left."

Stephanie tossed her hands in the air. "Isn't that just like a man? When you need them the most, they are *nowhere* to be found. I told you, Fiona, good husbands are hard to come by."

"Oh, yes, looks like Brian will be a real peach. You two deserve each other. Hope you don't have any peanut allergies, Brian."

Just then several boxes crashed to the cement floor, revealing Nathan's presence. He had Patsy by the collar. "Olly olly oxen free," he sang out.

"And there he is. I knew you couldn't be far." Brian raised his weapon. "It's too bad you and Ms. Quinn showed up here—"

"Honestly, you don't want to kill me. There's waaay too much paperwork involved," Nathan said.

"I won't be doing any. Stephie—"

"Didja hear that, Fiona? Brian uses pet names all the time. He called Tempest, T, and he calls Stephanie, Stephie. I still don't understand what the problem is with me calling you Fi." He raised his hands, feigning surrender. "Okay, okay, I do understand your aversion to poopylumps or Fifi, but I'm thinkin' Fi is a perfectly acceptable pet name."

"*Poopylumps?*" Brian said, taken aback. "Who calls their girlfriend poopylumps?"

"Don't ask."

Fiona's head was pounding. "At this point, Nathan, I don't care what you call me. I just want out of this basement. I need some fresh air." She looked at Brian, and then back to Nathan. Neither man seemed affected at all by the revolting reek of death. "I don't get it. Why isn't the smell bothering either of you?"

Nathan pointed to the area under his nose. "Vicks VapoRub."

Brian demanded, "Where did you get Vicks VapoRub?"

"From yours truly, Brian," Alex said. Brian spun around to stare down the business end of Alex's service revolver. "Annnd, you're under arrest, good buddy, for the murder of Tempest Belafonte." Speaking into a walkie-talkie on his Kevlar vest, Alex said, "Come on in, boys. Let's get them outta here."

Fiona laid her head against the wall. "Oh, good, does that mean we can go outside now? I think I'm gonna totally pass out if we don't."

"Just drop your gun, Brian. There's no way out of here. We've got the house surrounded," Alex said. Letting out a defeated sigh, Brian complied. "Oh, and I'm afraid you're under arrest too, Mrs. Friend, for the murder of Wyla Parkes and Dr. Richard Friend."

Officer Allen and several more police officers arrived at the top of the stairs to handcuff Brian. Alex reached passed Fiona for Stephanie's hand.

She placed her hand in his as if he were about to escort her into a dinner party. "I don't understand why you would arrest me, Alex. It was self-defense."

"Really? How do you figure, Mrs. Friend?" Nathan asked as he and Patsy made their way up the stairs.

"He was fooling around. I'd had enough. I had to protect my sanity, so I killed them," Stephanie explained as if she were giving directions to the nearest department store.

"Hm, I'm thinking that's more of a self-preservation defense than a self-defense defense," Nathan said. "Then again, ya never know how *creative* an attorney can get."

"Oh, that's right, I'm allowed one phone call. Alex, I need to call my attorney. He'll take care of this misunderstanding."

"Of course, Mrs. Friend. Hold that thought, this nice officer will take you to the station, and you can make that call." Alex shook his head as he passed Stephanie off to Officer Allen.

Nathan grabbed Fiona around the waist. "C'mon, honeybun, if I can call you honeybun, let's get you outside."

As they entered the living room police flooded into the house. Nathan led Fiona toward the front door with Patsy on their heels.

"Hey, Landry! I had Miss Quinn's car towed to the cottage—no charge," Alex called out. Nathan turned. Alex tossed a bite-sized KitKat bar to him.

Catching the small candy bar, Nathan began to remove the wrapper. "Thanks, but don't think I'm letting you off the hook, Belafonte. You owe me a steak dinner, and it looks like Fiona will be along as well."

Alex laughed. "My pleasure, only this time we'll just meet at the restaurant instead of that back road—although I must say, our plan worked out perfectly." He gestured toward Fiona. "Even with the glitch."

Nathan tossed the KitKat into his mouth. "Indeed it did, old chum—glitch and all. About seven o'clock, Ferrante's?"

"I'll be there."

Once Nathan had Fiona out of the house, he helped her to ease into a chair on the front porch. Brushing the back of his fingers across her cheek, he asked, "Are you gonna be okay?"

Fiona breathed in several deep breaths of fresh air. "I'm sure I will. Oh, Nathan, I feel just awful. I was so very wrong. I owe Alex a huge apology." She cocked her head to one side. "Wait a minute. What plan did you and Alex pull off perfectly?"

"The whole sting operation. You see, Kent found an app on Brian's phone that could be used to pre-schedule text messages, so even though his messages were worded differently than usual, the app showed us that the messages had been pre-set. Remember our trip to the carwash?"

"Yes…you said you got a movie."

"I did. When Brian said he hated the beach and sand, and you said his feet had been wet the night of Wyla's murder, I figured he needed to clean his car out from being at the beach with Tempest. Well, when I looked farther back on the tape, there he was cleaning his car out in the wee hours of the morning—the same day as Wyla's murder. Fast forward—and he did the same after Tempest's body had been discovered."

"Although I didn't actually have a solid motive at the time for his involvement in the two women's murders, I knew it would reveal itself along the way. But at the time, all the evidence was pointing at Alex, as Brian had it planned. So we simply played along. The only thing we weren't counting on was you. I *tried* to send you home so you would be out of harm's way. Officer Andy Allen called us and said that he'd overheard Brian talking with you and had told you about the meeting place. I was hoping you wouldn't actually show up, but was I surprised when you did show up with that crazy story about Harriet getting car sick? I think not. Again, we need to talk about boundaries—"

"But Alex pulled a gun on you."

"I'm sure the safety was on."

"You two sure were convincing—I truly thought Brian was innocent. I suppose I was the *glitch*. Oh, Nathan, I'm so sorry. But, what about Richard Friend? Did you suspect Stephanie had killed her husband?"

"No—that was a bonus murder, I'm afraid. Alex was well aware that Dr. Friend had a lot of flings, but he thought the man had gone to their summer home in the south, while Stephanie cooled off. But when you and I went into the Friend's home and she had all those candles burning, I knew she was trying to cover something up—something stinky."

"And you were right. I guess this is why you're the detective and I'm the kindergarten teacher."

Nathan kissed Fiona's forehead. "No worries. It all turned out for the best. Now you can come to dinner with Alex and me, but no guarantees on the belching and other bodily sounds."

Fiona chuckled. "I'm sure you'll both be on your best behavior." Patsy let out a whimper, then laid her head in Fiona's lap. She cupped the dog's face in her hands. "Oh, no, Nathan, what are we going to do about Patsy? With Stephanie being charged with murder, and Richard being one of her victims, the poor dog's pet-parents aren't able to care for her anymore. We can't let them take her to the pound."

Nathan swept a stray strand of hair away from Fiona's face, then he tickled Patsy's ears. "Don't worry about Patsy. I'll see to it that everything works out for the best. I promise. C'mon, let's get back to the cottage. You look wiped out. I think you'd better rest up before we meet Alex later on."

"Are we taking Patsy back to the cottage?"

"Of course we are. We certainly can't leave her here." Taking her hand, he hoisted Fiona from the chair.

"Well, I suppose it was a good thing that I still have the keys to the cottage. I don't just need a nap. I need a shower too," Fiona said.

As they made their way toward Nathan's SUV, and he helped Patsy into the back seat, Fiona let out a sigh of relief. She didn't know what Nathan was planning, but he always kept his word. Somehow she knew everything would work out for the beautiful Golden Retriever. With that in mind, Fiona was certain she'd be able to nap before dinner.

By the time six-thirty rolled around, Fiona was feeling refreshed. Not only had she managed a nap and a quick shower, but she and Nathan and the dogs had gone for a short walk along the beach—in the *opposite* direction from where the bodies had been found. Harriet and Patsy played and nipped at each other while jumping in and out of the surf.

"Too bad you didn't have a chance to go fishing," Fiona said.

"Next time," Nathan replied.

"Gawd, I hope not."

Nathan chuckled.

"Fiona...I gotta ask—is someone living in your house besides you?"

Yikes!

What was she supposed to say? She wasn't sure she was ready to share the secret of Evelyn with Nathan—or anyone else for that matter. Seriously...a ghost living in one's attic just sounds crazy. During the years that Evelyn had remained in the attic apartment after her death, she'd made herself known only to Fiona's mom,

Nancy, and to Fiona herself—not even her younger brother, Chad, had ever mentioned knowing about their grandmother's spirit. Fiona was certain that her mom had never told her father about Evelyn—Fiona wasn't exactly sure why. Perhaps because her father was a scoffer. Yeah, she could picture her father rolling his eyes at her mother and saying something like, *C'mon, Nancy, there's got to be a logical reason for the sounds you're hearing.* Her father tended to be very logical—a true pessimist at times. She didn't believe Nathan to be a scoffer. He seemed to be open to new ideas—more free thinking than her father. Then again, Evelyn wasn't exactly a new idea or a thought process—she was a spirit. How would he feel about a ghost living in her house? Especially a ghost who'd been playing tricks on him. More importantly, how would Evelyn feel about her telling the secret? She felt she needed to discuss divulging the secret with Evelyn first, although she'd never actually had a conversation with Evelyn. Just exactly what would that look like? Was she actually able to have a conversation with Evelyn?

Hm.

"Fiona—"

She snapped back into the moment when she realized he'd been trying to get her attention for a few seconds. She decided to buy some time. "You're at my house a lot, Nathan. How could someone else be living in my house without you knowing about it? I mean, where would they hide? Why would I hide them? Who on Earth would need to be hid? It's not like I hang out with criminals for crying out loud."

"I'm not talking about people—living breathing people anyway."

Double yikes.

"What kind of people are you talking about then?"

"Dead people, Fiona, dead people—ghosts, apparitions, spirits. Is there a ghost living in your house? Are you a ghost-whisperer?"

Now she had a problem.

He had out and out asked her. If she denied knowing about the ghost—she would be out and out lying. She was not good at that at all.

Fiona feigned a haughty laugh. "Me? A ghost whisperer? I don't think so—I...I never whisper at ghosts. I'd be more likely to run in the other direction. Really, Nathan, don't you think this conversation is a little silly?"

"Nope. But I'm not going to your house without you being there anymore until you come clean. Let's put the dogs away, it's time to meet Alex." He immediately turned away and started in the direction of the cottage. He called out, "C'mon, Patsy! C'mon, Harriet!"

Ho-boy. He seemed upset. Disappointed. Hokay, maybe it was time to come clean about Evelyn. Would her grandmother be okay with Nathan knowing or would she leave the house?

Fourteen

Ferrante's Winery and Ristorante was buzzing with diners. The wine was flowing, and the restaurant was filled with conversation and laughter, while the wait staff darted in and out of the kitchen. Fiona, Nathan, and Alex had been escorted to a table for six near the window looking out over the massive vineyards beyond the extensive patio. During the short wait for their table to be ready, Fiona had ordered a wine sampler and was slowly making her way through the sweet wines toward the drier varieties. Yum.

"There's only three of us, they should've given us a smaller table," Fiona pointed out when they arrived at their table.

The hostess was taken aback. She turned to Alex. "Your other guests won't be joining you?"

"It'll be fine, thank you," Alex told her.

With a lift of her shoulder, the hostess set a basket of bread and six menus on the table, then made her way back toward the reception area.

"Someone else is coming?" Fiona inquired.

"We'll see," Alex said. He scanned the reception area, then sat down.

"Poor Sam Ursler, I hope you released him," Fiona said, as she took a seat.

"He was released the moment I got back to the precinct. I didn't think you wanted to file any charges," Alex said. He lifted a dinner roll from the basket on the table.

"Goodness, no. I mean, I was annoyed that he tied me up, but I think he suffered enough by sitting in the jail cell for almost twenty-four hours." She glanced sheepishly at Nathan. "Well, I guess I've learned my lesson."

"Pfft," Nathan began. "I'll believe that when I see it…*Nancy*."

"Who's Nancy?" Alex asked.

"Fiona's mom, Nancy Quinn—the detective extraordinaire," Nathan replied, wryly.

"Uh, oh, domestic troubles," Alex snorted, and then he looked up. "Excuse me."

Fiona and Nathan directed their attention to the man and woman who were holding a small girl's hand while making their way through the throng of diners. Alex approached them and shook hands with the man. Fiona leaned in close to Nathan, "Isn't that Officer Allen?"

"Yes, that's his wife and daughter with him. His daughter is blind," Nathan explained.

"How sad. She looks to be about seven or eight."

"She's been blind since birth. They haven't been able to afford a guide dog for her—that's where Patsy comes in. I called Alex while you were napping. He said he knew someone who needed a good kind dog and thought Patsy would be a perfect fit for Officer Allen's little girl."

"How wonderful. I'm sooo happy." Fiona kissed Nathan's cheek. "You said everything would work out for Patsy and it did. Thank you, Nathan."

"Don't thank me, thank Alex. Patsy will have a loving forever home for sure. Take a look at that little girl—she's gonna fall head over heels with Patsy the moment they meet."

Fiona's heart was swelling with joy. "She sure will."

Leaving the lake was bittersweet. Especially after Officer Allen's little girl, Meg, was introduced to Patsy. She ran her tiny fingers over the Golden Retriever's eyes, snout, and fluffy ears, and Patsy took the opportunity to lick Meg's face. The little girl giggled in delight, threw her arms around Patsy and hugged her for all she was worth. Well, it was official—the two of them would be the best of friends for a very long time to come. Fiona and Officer Allen's wife got all teary-eyed over the new relationship.

Fiona rose early the next morning to take one more walk along the shore. Harriet reluctantly jumped down from her cozy nest, only to make a big production of yawning and stretching to send some kind of doggie message to her mistress that it was way too early to expect her to go for a walk. But once Fiona grabbed the leash from the hook and shook it in the Maltese's direction, Harriet scampered to the door, and when it was slid open, she scurried across the veranda and into the sand.

As Fiona strolled along the water's edge she thought about Wyla Parkes and how tragic her death was. Her readers would miss her. Noble Publishing? Well, they would most likely miss the revenue they would have collected from future books, but they would probably make a small fortune from her last work, Waves of Romance.

Fiona's mom had called the night before to inform her that Lester Crane had called her, and while Wyla had planned to self-publish the anthology, Noble would now acquire the work because Wyla was under contract with them, and she'd emailed the two manuscripts that were finished to Lester for him to read, therefore they became Nobel's property.

"Why on Earth would she do that?" Fiona asked her mother.

"Because it was what Wyla always did, I suppose. But, Lester asked me to edit the works because he knew that's what Wyla would've wanted. I think it's wonderful that he is respecting her wishes."

Although Waves of Romance was meant to be an anthology, it would now only be made up of two books because of Wyla's untimely death. And even though Fiona found the story she'd edited to be sappy—not her preference in reading material—she found the loss to romantic literature gravely unfortunate.

Instead of a blazing sunset over the tumbling water, she paused to watch the sun slowly rise, sending golden rays and a promise of a new day across the glistening tide. Fiona breathed it all in, and then headed back to the cottage to wake Nathan and drive back to Pittsburgh, back to her house on Oxford Street, back to her regular routine, and back to her ghostly roommate, Evelyn. She was ready—she couldn't wait.

"How nice was it that your captain gave you a few extra hours to get to work this morning? I suppose he figured you'd worked through the weekend—even though it wasn't a murder case in Pittsburgh, or it wasn't really your case at all, well, it was nice of him anyway," Fiona said as she pulled the door closed on the cottage and dropped the key into her purse.

"I guess," Nathan said.

Fiona hesitated. "Nathan…"

"Yeah?"

"Um…about that question you had…about the ghost in my house—"

"Yeah?"

"Well…" She searched the ground as if the right words would appear in the cement sidewalk. She trusted Nathan. She loved Nathan for cryin' out loud, but she simply wasn't ready to share Evelyn's secret with him—not yet anyway. Rather, she felt obligated to explain something there really was no explanation for. But how would she make it sound…sane?

Nathan brushed his fingers softly down her arm. Her eyes met his. He favored her with a svelte smile. "So what time is your mom's flight expected?"

Whatta guy.

"I'll be picking her up at the airport on my way home. Mom said they're shipping Wyla's body to Pittsburgh this afternoon. Her funeral services will be held on Wednesday."

"I'm gonna try to attend. Do you think your mom will bring the dogs with her?" Nathan asked as they made their way toward his SUV, with suitcases in hand, and Harriet merrily tagging along on a leash.

Fiona's parents had taken on five Yorkies when they retired and moved to Florida. Her mother claimed that the empty nest felt way too empty, and yet the dogs were easier to deal with than children—they rarely talked back, and their needs were more stress-free to tend to. Nancy's love of the Beatles prompted her to name each dog after a member of the popular group, except for one little Yorkie whom she'd named Keith.

Like Keith Richards of the Rolling Stones? Um, no. The dog had been named after Nancy's fiancé before she'd met Fiona's father, Garrett. After much fussing, and after a rough Christmas visit to Pittsburgh, the dog's name was changed.

Fiona said, "I'm not sure. Dad's not coming so if she brings any of the dogs it will more than likely be Sting—"

"The Yorkie formally known as Keith," they sang out in unison, and then shared a hearty chuckle.

Nathan pulled her close and kissed her lips. When he released the embrace he looked into her eyes and asked, "Now…before we hit the highway, I really need to know—in your opinion, which is better, Snickers or KitKat?"

Fiona tossed her head back in laughter. She favored him with an ornery grin. "That will remain a mystery, Detective Landry." With that, she kissed his cheek and she and Harriet trotted off toward her Mini Cooper parked just beyond his vehicle.

Over the hood of his SUV, Nathan called, "Well, all righty then…*poopylumps*."

END

Thank you for reading *Waves of Murder*. What's next for Fiona and Detective Landry?

Fiona and Detective Landry find themselves in the middle of a vintage murder during a wine tasting at one of Pittsburgh's premiere addresses, the Mansion on Fifth in the next installment of the Fiona Quinn Mysteries, *Tastes Like Murder*, coming very soon!

Have you read these other Fiona Quinn Mysteries? Check them out!

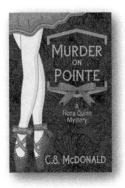 

**Note: *Murder on Pointe* is now available on audiobook!

For more information on the Fiona Quinn Mysteries or C.S. McDonald's children's books, please visit www.csmcdonaldbooks.com

For twenty-six years C.S. McDonald's life whirled around a song and a dance. She was a professional dancer and choreographer. During that time she choreographed many musicals and an opera for the Pittsburgh Savoyards. In 2011 she retired from her dance career to write. Under her real name,  Cindy McDonald, she writes murder-suspense and romantic suspense novels. In 2014 she added the pen name, C.S. McDonald, to write children's books for her grandchildren. Now she adds the Fiona Quinn Mysteries to that expansion. She decided to write the cozy mystery series for her young granddaughters, and has found that so many adults love them too.

Ms. McDonald resides on her Thoroughbred farm known as Fly by Night Stables near Pittsburgh, Pennsylvania with her husband, Bill, and her poorly behaved Cocker Spaniel, Allister.

You can learn more about C.S. McDonald and her books here: www.csmcdonaldbooks.com

Made in the USA
Middletown, DE
22 July 2019